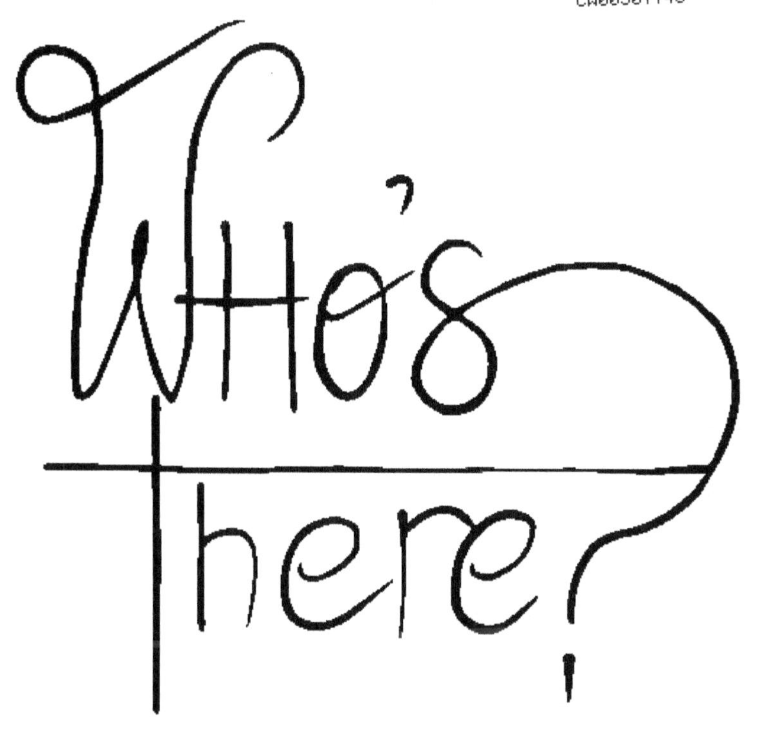

A Collection of Stories

DIMAS RIO

VELOX BOOKS
Published by arrangement with the author.

CONTENTS

WHO'S THERE?

Who's there, crouching like the moon behind the gray clouds?
Who's there, writhing about like a pouncing thunderbolt?
"Crawl out of the darkness, my child!"
called the Jungle to the restless Hunchback.
"Don't you know? Darkness is my blood,"
howled the cursed Hunchback.
The Jungle cracked a smile, red and ripe.
"Then, you are my beloved."

The cold and salty ocean breeze caressed the face of the wavy-haired man, sitting with his arms folded on the table. His gaze ran around the evening sky which veiled the universe, but neither the fizz of the waves crashing on the beach, nor the drizzle of the rain filling the air could make him feel at one with nature; he still felt like an outsider looking in. Forever a tourist on Earth. A cactus in the snow. A bat in the daytime. An anomaly.

"Adam?"

The voice interrupting his reverie belonged to Angga, a man of his peers, sitting right across from him. Adam shifted his gaze toward Angga. The stocky, dark-skinned thirty-year-old was sitting next to Farah, an exotic-looking woman whose cascade of jet-black hair fell over her brows.

"Where's Gita?" he heard Angga asking.

Waving his cellphone, Adam let his friend know that he had sent Gita a text; "She'll be here soon."

Adam turned his gaze back to the shore, a mere eight meters from the beach bar where he currently sat. A few foreign tourists were seen making their way around the pools of rainwater forming in the holes on the street. Some looked to have been ahead of the game—with their raincoats and umbrellas—to anticipate the November weather on the fifteen-square-kilometer island, which lay at the center of the archipelago. Others didn't even bother to cover themselves from the rain shower. Many of the women around him looked comfortable jogging and cycling in their everyday clothes, unprotected from the weather. He heard Angga teasing that it could be his last week to freely lay his eyes on the voluptuous bodies roaming the street before him—his friend's remark made his stomach churn. Still, in the same joking manner, he replied that was exactly why he had asked his fiancée to take her time following them down to the bar.

"So, are you really ready or not?" he heard Angga asking him again, after their laughter had subsided.

"Well, I have to be," said Adam, before he drained his glass of light-green cocktail. He liked it when the ice cubes clinked and slid together toward his lips, surrendering to the control of his hand. The burning sensation from the vodka drink managed to dissolve the lump which had been blocking his throat.

"Why do you say that as if you don't have a choice?" asked Angga. Then, with a conspiratorial sidelong glance at his wife, "You know what, babe? I don't think this boy is ready." Farah seemed to agree with her husband's hypothesis.

Adam knew that his best buddy was just teasing him, as usual. He also presumed that whatever he said in response would be quickly countered by a witty remark from his friend, which would further drive him into a corner—he believed that police characters in television shows used this trick to make their suspects slip up, become defensive and finally appear as guilty criminals. He hated those characters. But, of course, he didn't reveal this sentiment to his friend.

"Well, it's no different to when *you* were getting married," Adam retorted, and saw his friend's face twitch in panic.

Impulsively, Angga tried to hide his horror by laughing. His voice became incredibly shrill as he replied, "*I* was the one who wanted to rush *her* into marriage! *She* may have been the one who felt forced to marry *me*!"

Adam laughed along with his friend, mostly because he was relieved that he had been able to stop his friend's fast train of jokes, before it crashed through the hidden cavities of his soul, where creatures like anxiety, shame and fear resided. These creatures were undetectable by the senses, but they continued to squirm; to pester; to crave, like a snake. Adam had always been reluctant to acknowledge their existence to anyone—even his best friend, and especially his fiancée. To him, these bugs were like embarrassing family members who deserved to be locked up, behind walls, far away from the light of day; to be left alone until they died and rotted. But they never did. Hiding them seemed only to have made them flourish; he could feel them, starting to crawl out through his pores, his eyeballs, from the mucous membrane of his throat, spilling out over his lips. He feared his fear so much, but he didn't want to kill it instantly. He felt that the fear was what had been shaping him, making him the way he was; he owed his life to his fear. He wanted to keep feeding those creatures, yet prayed for them to choke on their own meal and die.

Adam ordered a bottle of tequila from the bar. He saw surprise in his friends' faces when the gleaming bottle of the golden liquor, along with three shot glasses and a plateful of lime slices, landed on the wooden table by their elbows.

"Seriously?" Farah said, raising her eyebrows.

Adam dismissed her with a wave of his hand. He asked the two to consider tonight the substitute for his bachelor party. The only difference was that he would pay for everything, on the condition that they finished any drink he ordered from the bar.

"So, apparently last night wasn't enough, huh?" asked Farah, in complete disbelief.

Adam knew exactly what the woman was implying, though he couldn't actually recall most of what had happened the night before. And when she said "last night", she was actually referring to the hours between two and seven this morning—or, what Adam had *believed* was seven a.m., for the sun had been glaring in his eyes and roasting his entire body. He vaguely remembered how his body had felt, like it was shrouded in suffocating fumes. He had been sweltering in his own skin…

§

I wish I could skin myself, Adam groaned to himself, tottering to the side of the street, aiming for the shade next to a pile of garbage. Like a vampire, desperately seeking refuge from the sun's deadly lick.

He could feel two hands on his shoulders, catching him from an ungainly nose dive, and he heard Angga saying, "Let's go home, let's go home," repeatedly, like a mantra, as he was helped to maneuver down the street, avoiding several menacing-looking men in front of a pub, where the four from the city had spent their time the night before. Angga's unsettled voice sounded ludicrous to his ears, maybe because he had never seen his friend so nervous in all of the years he had known him.

Through the hundreds of fluttering wings playing tricks on his eyes, he managed to catch a glimpse of Farah and Gita hurriedly walking past him. Wrapped in an ethnic printed cloth, each of his fiancée's strides looked determined and intense, as if wanting to leave her alcohol-reeking husband-to-be as quickly as possible. Farah put her arm around her friend and gave her a gentle squeeze, as if to send her an unspoken message: *Everything will be alright*—a phrase which, to Adam, seemed to make all who said it end up as liars.

§

Adam looked down at the knuckles of his hands, which were red and swollen. The sting he felt served as a reminder of what he had done just a few hours ago. Fragments of what had happened that night and early in the morning flashed inside his head, like dim images projected onto a dark wall.

He remembered the part in the morning when he had rubbed his face with all of his might, in front of the mirror above the sink, to wipe away the annoying twitches which were suddenly invading his facial muscles. He had let the water rush from the open tap, hoping that the sound of it running down the drain could help slow down the pounding of his heart, which—based on the sluggish feeling he was suffering with—seemed to have betrayed his body and transformed into a blood-sucking organ. He also wished that his hard rubbing could somehow scrape away the face of the stranger looking back at him from the mirror. The face was as white as limestone, with red vines of veins creeping across its eyes, making them look infected. But, when he lowered his hands, the face in the mirror was still there; that pair of red eyes was still watching him. He knew that, no matter how hard he rubbed, the face wouldn't go anywhere; it had now become his.

§

Angga's voice snapped his soul back to the body which had been sitting in the bar, on the remote island, thousands of miles away from his life in the capital city. A life which was about to make him vow that he would love only his wife, accept all of her shortcomings and listen to all of her troubles.

Every morning.

Every night.

Every day.

For as long as they both shall live. Until death do them part.

Just thinking about how the promise—which was supposedly mere ritual—could bind him as tightly as the piece of metal which would adorn his ring finger one week from now was reason enough for him to pour the golden, yellow liquid from the bottle into the shot glass, and drain it in one swift series of movements.

This fluent act was countered by a protest from Angga and Farah—the kind usually exclaimed in unison by passengers in a car, when the driver goes too fast, or the car is involved in a near-miss, following a too-sharp turn. Farah asked him if he thought alcohol was a good idea, especially after what had happened that morning.

Adam dismissed her criticism by saying that they were both overreacting; he wasn't the type to fall into the same hole, just hours after the first time. Truth be told, Adam didn't believe a word he was saying, either.

Both Angga and Farah looked like they were witnessing something unusual. Angga immediately asked him the predicted and dreaded question. "What's really happening, Adam?"

Adam could feel the creatures inside him stirred to life, as if awakened by a mantra. The scaled, egg-shaped head looked up, hissed, and got ready to tighten its twist around his heart, which was now pounding industriously.

But, like the billions of other people in the world, Adam knew that the answer to this question was more than simple; it was an auto-reply. "Nothing," Adam responded, as calmly as on the days when he had spoken the truth. It seemed like those days would soon be permanent history for him.

But, of course, the couple in front of him would not stop firing him with questions. As if trying to string together a limerick, Angga shot him with the second stanza. "Is everything alright with Gita?"

Adam responded in a similar manner, though this time more agilely, like in spontaneous exclamation—or, perhaps, the opposite: a *rehearsed* exclamation. Hearing the artificial response once more spill out of his own mouth made him want to roar, vomit and cry, all at the same time. He felt like a hollow shell covering a vacuum. There were no traces of a civilized human inside: no conscience; no courage; no guilt.

But, like bubbles which formed as water started to boil, a splinter of truth escaped from his mouth. "I guess she's still mad," Adam admitted.

His two friends made sympathetic faces. Angga asked if Adam had tried apologizing to his fiancée.

"Of course I have," he replied, trying hard not to lose his temper.

Instantly, his body felt like it was a time machine, bringing him back to his hotel room…

§

The image which materialized before him, right at that moment, was of his own two hands, clasped as if in prayer. The view of the gold band encircling his left ring finger sent the contents of his stomach to his throat.

The sight of the wood-grain pattern on the vinyl made him realize that he was staring down so intensely, it was as if he were trying to turn the floor into a door-way, which would take him to another world—anywhere but this room.

But the floor didn't turn into a door. And, his two hands were not clasped in prayer; they were simply clutching each other, to keep his body from disintegrating.

Maybe it's better if I cease to exist.

The raw pain in his swollen hands not only reminded him that life had not left his body, but also confirmed his conviction that the world would never grant miracles to a cursed man like him. Miracles were given only to divine saints, who had all lived thousands of years ago.

Like a rat hiding from the snake's pursuit, Adam looked up in terror. The screen of the tube T.V., which was glowing luminously before him, displayed a show's host naming and shaming local celebrities, with great dedication. Adam couldn't hear a word of it, though; the only words nestling against his eardrums were those of his own disgrace, screamed by Gita:

"I'm not like my mother and father, who you can fool into thinking that you're the most pious, gentle, obedient human being. I know what's really behind your mask: just another spoilt man; a hypocrite who acts like a righteous person.

"If you're not ready to tie the knot, if you still want to fool around, be a man about it and say it to my face... and my parents'. You've got nothing to lose if we cancel our wedding; you haven't spent a dime.

"Don't you dare try and calm me down! When you made a scene at the bar last night, you weren't even listening to me."

§

On autopilot, Adam grabbed the glass bottle in front of him and poured the tequila into his shot glass. He jerked his head backward and gulped it down. The fire spreading through his throat instantly brought his soul back to the body sitting in the beachside bar, with Angga and Farah.

"I think you'd better give Gita a call," he heard Angga saying.

Adam replied that he had called her before they arrived at the bar.

Farah, who could smell a lie like a vulture, from kilometers away, looked incredulous. She stared at him for a moment before saying, "That was an hour ago. Why don't I call her?"

"No," said Adam, a little too abruptly to sound like the polite turndown he had intended. Seeing the alarmed faces of his friends, he quickly added, "Let me call her," in what he hoped was a calm tone. He dialed his fiancée's number and pressed the cellphone to his ear.

With very little delay, he was talking to Gita. Words came out of his mouth in rapid succession, as if communicating with his wife-to-be was as painful as standing on shards of glass, barefoot. In less than two minutes, he had already said what he had to say. "Are you coming or not? We've been here for an hour. How much longer? Okay, let me know when you're on your way."

Adam ended the conversation, telling his two friends that Gita was working on a sudden assignment from her office, and would be on her way as soon as she had wrapped things up; "She just got it sent by email."

"How much longer?" asked Farah.

"Dunno," replied Adam, once again pouring the alcohol into his shot glass, "she'll probably need some time. You're sure you don't want any food or drinks?"

Almost in unison, both Angga and Farah told him that they were sure.

For a while, none of them spoke. The crashing waves, less than ten meters from where they were sitting, now sounded ten times farther than that. The loud party music playing, which usually gripped their heads like the tentacles of an octopus, now sounded as forgettable as the background music in a shopping center. Nearby conversations, usually up close and personal, were transformed into nothing more than pantomimes. The silence made Adam feel like he was in the spotlight. Scrutinized. Talked about.

He took another gulp of his drink, letting the ethanol dissolve in his blood, control his mind and whisper its satanic propositions. Gradually, everything felt easier; nothing to worry about. He believed that what had happened could no longer be changed, and what had not happened was only a figment of his imagination.

Adam could see that Farah was restless. She mumbled to her husband, loud enough for Adam to hear, "I'm going to the ladies' room," then she left their table.

Even in his not-too-sober state, Adam could accurately read that Farah didn't really need to go; she wanted to call her bestie, who was supposedly finishing up an urgent assignment in her hotel room, and would most likely ask her the same questions Adam had done three minutes ago, on the phone.

What a waste of time, Adam thought, wryly. But he knew that his friends had started to doubt every word coming out of his mouth tonight. Adam felt the outer layer of his skin, which had been shielding his body, start to wrinkle, shed and die, revealing the shivering, exposed glands. But he couldn't do anything. He could only hope that the pillars of this Earth would soon collapse, so that he could be buried underneath them.

"Are you two going back tomorrow?" he heard his friend asking, to fill the void.

"We hope so," he replied.

Angga was saying that Adam and his fiancée should not have come on this trip together, so close to their wedding day—the bride-to-be was supposed to be in seclusion. "People say it's prohibited," explained Angga; "*pamali!*"

"You sound like my future in-laws," Adam retorted. "Anyway, didn't you two travel to the U.K. a week before you were supposed to marry?"

"Yeah, but we didn't quarrel like you two," Angga chuckled.

Adam dismissed the comment by blaming "pre-wedding jitters". Angga responded to these empty words with a ceremonious laugh, then said, "I think you should go get her. She's probably still angry."

Once again, Adam attempted to dismiss his friend's advice. "You know her. If she says she's coming, she's coming."

Besides, thought Adam, *it's a waste of energy*. And, he felt his energy had already been drained because of the "incident"—the incident which had happened this afternoon.

Adam shifted his gaze to where the waves met the shore, not too far from where he was. Every inch of the horizon was now painted in thick, black ink, making the island seem like it was in the eye of a storm. At that moment, the waves no longer sounded like they were crashing; to him, they sounded like they were gushing.

§

His eyes were suddenly raw; he wiped them with two wet hands. He looked down and was startled to see an ivory-white ceramic sink before him, overflowing. He could see the black rubber plug at its bottom, motionless, like a tadpole trapped in a trench; dead and forgotten.

When he looked up, a pair of red eyes staring back at him made him jolt in surprise. It took him a moment to realize that he was back in the hotel's bathroom, and that the red-eyed creature staring defiantly at him from the mirror was himself. His *real* self, who only appeared when the whole world was not looking.

Adam gripped the edges of the sink, as if trying to push back the urge to drown himself in it. A ridiculous notion, he knew, but Gita's insulting words were floating in the air, permeating into the locked bathroom like toxic gas, making him want to hold his face under the water.

"You don't need to apologize. Had our wedding ever been important to you, you wouldn't have behaved like that. You've just never respected me as your fiancée; I'm grateful that I got to see your true nature now. I wouldn't want somebody like you for a husband.

"So, congratulations, from now on you can drink all you want, do drugs, and fool around with any woman you like. Here's your ring. Send my regards to your family."

"Wait," Adam had tried to counter her, but his hoarse voice was drowned out by the sound of the water gushing from the tap, which echoed throughout the whole bathroom. As he turned toward the door, the swing of his hand knocked an open plastic bottle off of

the edge of the sink, the clonazepam plunging into the pool of water forming on the floor; white pills flew out, dancing in the ripples.

"Gita, wait!" Adam called to her again. Half-running to the door, he almost slipped, but managed to grab the door handle and pull it open. He left a trail of wet footprints in the hall of the room, some forty-three square meters. He observed the room like a bat, flying over the bed, the desk, the porch and the pair of lounge chairs.

There was no sign of Gita. At once, Adam ran toward the front door and stepped outside. He called his fiancée's name, this time louder than before. Though every corner of the floor's corridor echoed his call, just as he had expected, there was no reply. Adam knew that he had to run after his fiancée, to proclaim many varieties of the word "sorry" to her. To hold her. Kiss her. Kneel at her feet.

He would play any role to stop her canceling their wedding; he couldn't bear to think of the scandal, the whispering, and the questions which would surely be directed at him when he got back to the city, once the news had spread. His stomach tightened as he pictured himself having to return to his cramped apartment, cruising the streets in his old car, missing the opportunity to flaunt the joyful moment in front of everyone who had ever known him, and being made the subject of water-cooler gossip amongst his colleagues.

He was quickly yanking open the wardrobe beside the door, looking for the shoes he had put there earlier, when his eyes zeroed in on something sitting at the bottom of the wardrobe. He crouched down in front of the open wardrobe to examine the object closer—a bright-red leather bag, with a gold-plated zipper, slightly open; he knew for sure that it was Gita's handbag. He assumed that she must have been so preoccupied with anger she had accidentally left without her bag.

But then he frowned when his fingers found a purse containing his fiancée's I.D. card, credit cards and money. He also found a rectangular object wrapped in silicone casing, which he immediately recognized as Gita's cellphone.

A sudden chuckle escaped his mouth when he pictured his fiancée stomping back to the hotel, grumpily remarking that she had forgotten her bag. Then, like some cheesy rom-com, Adam would reply that it was not only her bag she had left, but also her heart; in his mind's eye, he saw that Gita wouldn't be able to help but smile. He would then cup her oval face in his hands, and he would apologize to her for the hundredth time, promising to be the husband she had always dreamed of, while Gita would stare deep into his eyes with conviction. Then, they would hold each other close, forgetting everything that had happened. The vision was so real that he believed everything would be just fine in no time.

The flow of water tickling his soles shifted his gaze downward. A ripple of water had seeped underneath the bathroom door, like a severe case of bleeding which couldn't be stopped. He quickly stood up to go turn off the tap, then stopped abruptly, as he caught something from the corner of his eye which he had previously missed. Next to the wooden cabin stood an orange suitcase. The light from the setting sun filtered through the porch window, made the scene look like an old photograph. From the way the handle had been pulled up, and the zipper sliders were in the locked position, he could see that the suitcase was ready to go.

But it hadn't gone anywhere.

Adam walked over to the suitcase, each step accompanied by a splash, as his feet came into contact with the water. He lifted the suitcase with both hands. It was heavy; he knew that all of Gita's stuff must be inside.

His vision suddenly began to blur. The entire room felt like it was melting as the colors blended into one another. He massaged his temples until his eyesight recovered, but he couldn't get rid of the waves of nausea which were rising inside his body. He knew something wasn't right, but he couldn't quite pin it down. It made him want to bang his head against a rock, hoping that an explanation—the sliver of a story, or the chip of a memory—would bounce out of the void inside his head.

Adam tried to logically deduce what had happened from the scene before him. All of her stuff was still here. She had already said that she would be gone this afternoon, yet her stuff was still here. He wracked his brain. Surely she wouldn't be able to get home without her I.D. card. And he knew that she would never leave the room without her handbag, let alone her cellphone.

But she was also not here.

The water had now flooded the entire room; he could feel the weak, wet current caressing his ankles. It started to seep into the table legs and creep up the corners of the bedsheet and comforter, which touched the floor.

He shot his eyes back toward the wardrobe, across the bathroom. The side with its door open still showed Gita's leather bag, which was now surrounded by water. The door to the other side was still shut. He remembered that his fiancée had hung some of her clothes there, but it should be empty now, with all of her clothes neatly folded inside the orange suitcase before him.

Should be.

But, his mind had started to generate ideas which bewildered him. The only defense he had against the revolting images was a scornful laugh at himself, no matter how artificial it sounded in his head.

How much longer will you live like this? Adam jeered at himself. *You're a thirty-year-old man, getting married in a week; it's time to stop living inside your head.*

The self-rebuke managed to ignite a little courage, buried in the pit of his soul. He took a deep breath and a step forward. Reaching for the wardrobe handle, he yanked it open. The wooden door easily folded outward, roughly slapping the air, as its hinges screeched, revealing to Adam the secrets it had been hiding: a portable safe-deposit box and four clothes-hangers calmly swinging inside seemed to laugh at Adam's paranoid state.

He rested his back against the wall, staring at the now entirely open wardrobe. Empty, as if the only one creature haunting this room had been him. He let out a bitter laugh, thinking about it.

Don't worry, Adam, you haven't gone mad. You arrived on this island with your fiancée and your two friends two days ago. Not just one, but many hotel staff can confirm that. Gita's suitcase and handbag, that you can clearly see, also prove that.

The steady flow of water coming under the bathroom door tapped his ankles, bringing him back to reality, and he suddenly remembered that he needed to turn off the tap before the entire room turned into a lake. He turned, stepped into the bathroom, reached for the thin lever above the sink and pushed it down to stop the water. In an instant, the room became silent, like a music player suddenly losing its power. The only sound he heard was water being sucked into the drain at the corner of the bathroom. Softly, beautifully calming... Like the sound of wind-chimes clinking together on a porch.

He had just pulled the rubber plug in the bottom of the sink, to empty the basin, when he noticed his plastic bottle—which had a few moments ago contained the magic anxiety-relief pills—bobbing up and down on the floor. He immediately picked it up, trying to rescue what was left inside, but all he found was something of a chalky solution and a soaking wet paper label, describing the ingredients and usage instructions. He threw the bottle at the bin beside the sink, but his hurl only sent it against the side of the metal receptacle, before it bounced back onto the floor. He didn't bother to pick it up again. Truthfully, he wasn't too upset about the wasted magic pills; he had more in his bag.

Gita never suspected that he was an addict; as far as she knew, they were for his migraines. At least, she'd never had any suspicion until a couple of hours ago, when she seemed to have burnt her last nerve and blew fire at him, through a combination of screaming, shouting and punching, so brutal and gruesome that he'd thought she was possessed by some entity; a puppet breathed into life by a mantra.

I have to find her, Adam willed himself, inwardly. *She must be somewhere around the hotel.* His best bet was that Gita had gone to see Farah somewhere on the island, to tell her everything that had happened this afternoon. The idea, being judged by the people closest to him, made him anxious. A dirty secret coming to light was his biggest fear. But he knew it was too late for him to stop its rotten odor from reaching their noses. The only thing he could do now was call Angga and Farah to make sure that Gita was with them.

He was just about to head out of the bathroom, to get his cellphone, when he stepped on the plastic pill-bottle on the floor, slipped and lost his balance, landing on his elbow, which knocked the bathtub. He roared like a trapped animal; the pain shooting upward, from his elbow to the top of his head, felt like the shock from an electric eel.

He cursed and leant his head against the translucent vinyl curtain hiding the ceramic bathtub, then let out a long laugh, as if just having heard some hilarious joke. He laughed until he was out of breath, thinking how satisfied Gita would be to see him now. Drunk, paranoid and drenched, like someone just took a leak on him. How relieved she must be that she no longer needed to lower her status by marrying him; God must love her so much that He had protected her from a lowly creature like Adam.

He closed his eyes, trying to push back the venomous ideas which often paralyzed his conscience. He knew he should be grateful that Gita was not in this room, to see him in his current state. He still had time to freshen up before going to Angga's room to fetch his fiancée—if she was there.

He groaned in pain when he tried to push himself up, leaning on the edge of the tub.

The image projected by the light onto his cornea made him freeze.

Through the translucent curtain, with bead-like water droplets clinging it, he could see that the bathtub was filled with water. The ceramic's color and the room's lighting made it look almost green, like the color of a lake. In the tub was a pair of female legs—like mannequin parts being washed downstream.

He blinked, hoping that his eyes had deceived him.

Alas, for the first time that day, his retina wasn't sending a delusional image to the neurons in his brain. He knew that what he saw was real—as real as the cold eyes staring back at him from beneath the watery sheet.

He crawled along the side of the bathtub, his eyes locked onto the face which would forever be stuck in its stunned expression, the face of his bride-to-be. She lay at the bottom of the bathtub. Her body was rigid and swollen; the skin of her fingers and soles were wrinkled, as if she had aged overnight; her eyeballs looked flat, like ink drops. Lifeless.

But she still looked angry.

Adam felt his whole body crumble. His stomach felt like it was tightly wrapped in convulsions, ready to spurt out the bile inside it. He gasped for air, trying to steal every liter of the remaining oxygen in the room. Pushing his body away from the tub, he crawled on his hands and knees along the wet floor.

But those goggle eyes kept following his every movement. Hunting him. Cussing him.

He didn't even hear the scream coming out of his mouth.

§

Adam was staring at his swollen, throbbing hands when Farah arrived back at the table, where he and Angga sat. "Gita didn't answer my call."

"Didn't you say you were going to the toilet?" Adam countered, exposing the woman's lie.

Farah went on to explain that she had called Gita afterward, because she was worried about her friend. Adam asked her why she felt the need to call his wife-to-be, when he had already explained that she was trying to finish work at the hotel, and would be along soon.

"So what if I called her? Is she not allowed to talk to other people?" Farah quickly retorted in a sharp tone.

His heart was beating faster. He felt like he was being dissected alive. The imaginary bandage he had been trying to wrap around his entire body was slowly beginning to come loose and unravel, revealing scabs and abscesses, which Farah seemed able to sniff out.

"Why do you have to meddle with other people's business?" Adam had intended to keep this to himself—as usual. But this time his thought managed to flick out through the narrow gap between his lips, like a snake's forked tongue.

Adam now watched Angga react, warning his friend not to speak to his wife that way; Angga glared at him, as if building a physical shield for his wife—something Adam could no longer do for Gita. It made Adam want to scrape the look off of his friend's face, to make it as hollow as his own. He wanted to push Angga with all of his might; to strangle him, so that he also felt the pain. It wouldn't be his first time, anyway.

"Teach your wife not to stick her nose into other people's business."

"Teach your mouth to be more respectful to women! You want to make a scene again? Here? I'm sure everyone here is used to parading drunken tourists to the local police station."

The words were potent enough to make Adam freeze. He knew that he had to stay below the radar of the police—and anyone who might be a potential witness. He could only glare back at his friend, as if he had been betrayed; exiled.

Certain that his cursed hands would soon obey the command of his emotions to hit Angga over the head with something, Adam decided to walk out of the bar, leaving Angga and his wife behind.

It was already late, as Adam mounted the bicycle he had parked in front of the bar. The dark-green, iron-framed vehicle had been lent by the hotel where Adam and Gita were staying, being the main mode of transportation on the island, aside from horse-drawn cart. Pushing his feet against the gravelly ground, he tried to pedal the bicycle, but kept losing balance, his two feet always landing back where they started. Adam laughed, imagining all the pairs of eyes, including those of Angga and Farah, watching and mocking him from the bar. *Look at that man! He's so drunk, he can't even ride his bicycle!*

He focused his mind on his two hands, holding the rubber-padded handlebars, and his two feet, one on the pedal and one on the gravel, trying to dismiss the eyes he imagined were judging him. When he felt strong enough, he pushed his right foot against the gravel path, stepped onto the black aluminum pedals and cycled until both of the wheels spun forward. He took the bicycle to a run along the heavenly island, whose eternity depended on mortal beings who knew nothing but hunger and thirst.

Adam fixed his gaze ahead as the bicycle glided forward. The road to his hotel, two kilometers from the hustle and bustle of the island, was sparsely populated.

The scenery was dominated by the moonlight, its source at the center of the darkened sky, the gravelly and sandy path, and coconut groves owned by the locals. Once in a while, he saw locals and other tourists walking and biking in the opposite direction. Once, he thought he saw someone who looked like Gita, passing him by on a bicycle, heading in the direction he had come from. He immediately turned away; he didn't dare to look closer.

He pedaled his bicycle faster, not wanting to see his fiancée's face again that night.

But, like a sneer from the grave, he immediately saw a wet female riding a bike toward him. Her eyes were wide, like Gita's had been, when he drowned her in the water with a vengeance. She wore the same clothes Gita had worn, as she struggled to break free from his grip: a pink, sleeveless blouse and a pair of floral-print beach shorts. The woman's skin was swollen and peeling, as if she had been sleeping under water for hours.

As he saw the woman on the bike coming closer toward him, his heartbeat sounded like a series of rhythmic explosions in his ears—so loud that he felt his blood vessels would burst, letting the content spill out of all five senses. The figure coming toward him grew clearer, unveiled by the pale moonlight. He could see the woman's black hair was wet and disheveled, sticking to the side of her face, like shiny, coiling eels. Her blue lips framed an open mouth, which looked like it wanted to holler something.

Adam stopped pedaling. He didn't want to cross paths with the figure. Just thinking about this woman gliding past him, their shoulders inches apart, made him want to jump off of the bicycle and run from the path, as if it were made of piles of earthworms.

Still, his eyes were fixed on the face, now five meters away from where he had stopped. The woman's face was blue—not because of the moonlight, he guessed, but because the face was drowned. The eyeballs, staring from sockets which no longer blinked, didn't appear shiny; they looked dead, both still fixed on him. They were like opposite magnetic poles, finding each other.

Her mouth looked like it was about to say something. But, no; when the face was only a meter from him, he realized at once that the orifice was spilling something: water. He could hear her gasping for air, her squeals high-pitched and piercing his ears, followed by the sounds of choking and water spluttering out of her mouth. He realized that the woman who had stolen Gita's face was dying. Just like his wife-to-be had done, hours ago, when he held her underwater for six minutes.

A splash of water coming from the cursed mouth landed on Adam's face, and he instantly jumped off of his bike, as if he had just been slapped with dirt. He let his bicycle fall to the ground and rubbed his face in a frenzy, as if trying to rid his skin of the filth.

When he opened his eyes, his fiancée's face had already been replaced by that of a regular female tourist, who looked at him with astonishment as she passed him on her bicycle.

Adam couldn't catch his breath. He stared at the tourist, her clothes now completely different from Gita's, her body not looking at all like it had been submerged underwater, as she glided away with her bike, toward the darkness of the night.

The sudden ring of a cellphone broke the silence, jolting him into action. In a panic, he searched inside the pocket of his pants for his cellphone. Then, he decided not to answer and let it ring; he could already guess who was calling: it must have been Angga, calling to go off on him. His friend would swear that he would beat Adam up if he was ever again disrespectful to his wife. He would then tell Adam not to talk to him or his family ever again, and he would wish for Gita to realize soon what kind of man she was about to marry.

The destructive notions circling inside Adam's head did not burden him. He knew that the world had started to shudder uncomfortably at him. He could only surrender, waiting for nature to conspire against him and finish him off.

He remounted his bicycle. The never-ending ring of the cellphone in his pocket chattered away with the cooing of the nocturnal animals, escorting him back to his hotel.

Adam parked his bicycle at the iron bar in front of the hotel lobby, alongside the bicycles of other guests. His head felt like it was being weighed down by sacks of sand. He knew that the venomous liquid he had drained at the bar earlier was now arrogantly showing off its efficacy—even more powerful than that he had felt the night before. He limped past the lobby and the ground-floor corridor, ignoring the evening greetings from the white-uniformed hotel staff, who were well-versed in the unfriendly attitudes of urban tourists.

The corridor of the two-story hotel looked deserted as he walked along it. The dim light from the ethnic-styled chandelier floating on the ceiling seemed to confirm that the place would soon be dozing off. The overlapping whispers, heard from behind locked doors along the corridor, the whistle of the ocean breeze in his ears, and the crashing waves, which seemed to be the sacred direction faced by every lodging on this island, composed a serenade that made his eyelids feel heavy. He supposed that he was under the influence of something—something only heard through the ears of the wicked.

Adam was climbing up the stairs to his room on the second floor, when once again his cellphone rang. The tune was too cheerful, too joyful; it felt like it was violating the norms, like someone bursting into laughter in the middle of a funeral.

Looks like Angga is desperate to unleash his rage at me, Adam thought to himself. He wasn't surprised that his friend was calling him repeatedly; he understood how hard it must have been for Angga not to be able to spit out his swearing, cursing and other profanities, holding them inside in the name of good manners. He decided to give his friend what he needed: release. He reached into his pocket and took out the singing cellphone. When the palm-sized screen was facing up at him, from his hand, he was stunned.

He blinked, trying to send away the hellish illusion, which he assumed was being brewed by his slow, weakened mind. But, the series of letters written on his cellphone's screen did not change, no matter how many times he blinked. The name on the screen wasn't Angga's, but Gita's.

Nausea traveled fast, from his stomach to his throat, like magma. His heart was again restless, beating wildly, as if struggling to break free from his ribcage. His body wobbled, as though he was standing on the deck of a swaying ship, in the high tide.

The remaining splinter of his common sense tried to grasp what was happening. *It must be Angga or Farah, using Gita's cellphone to scare me.*

The hypothesis was quickly dismissed: he knew that Angga and Farah couldn't have gotten their hands on Gita's cellphone; it was still inside his fiancée's handbag, in the wardrobe, where Adam last saw it. He also knew that no one could have stepped into the room, since he had left for the bar to create an alibi.

He finally arrived at the closed door to his room, his hand still holding the ringing cellphone. Gita's name could still be read clearly on the screen, flashing like a child's toy. He was motionless. He couldn't open the door.

Quietly, he stuck his ear to the door's surface. He didn't know what he longed to hear. Footsteps on the floor? The soft rustle of the mattress supporting a human body? The squeaking of a chair being pulled out of its hiding place, underneath the desk? The only sound he heard was silence. It scared and relieved him at the same time.

A part of him wished that there was somebody in his room: perhaps housekeeping staff, checking his room, following a complaint from another guest of water dripping from the second floor. It might have even been the staff who called him, using Gita's cell-phone.

Or maybe there was somebody else in this hotel who knew what he had done. He suddenly felt dizzy. He must have left a lot of clues and traces of evidence while drowning his fiancée in the bathtub.

If any of his guesses were right, he knew he couldn't be in this hotel, or even on this island, for much longer; whoever went inside his room would have certainly seen the stiff and blackened body in the bathtub.

The cellphone in his hand finally stopped ringing. The screen dimmed then went black, making the cutting-edge device no more useful than a brick.

His ears were still trying to catch every trace of sound coming from inside the room, but his auditory nerves could only send a signal of silence to his brain. He gave up.

He tried to take a deep breath, but the air seemed reluctant to enter his lungs. His body felt heavy, as if gravity had been pulling him downward. It occurred to him to go inside the room, jump into the bed and sleep, but his half-awake instinct told him to get the hell out of the place.

Right at that moment, the door suddenly opened slowly, followed by a long whine, which sounded like it was emitted from ancient, porous joints. Beyond the doorframe, pitch-black darkness nurtured every shape and rounded every corner; the blackness flooding the room looked permanent, like a burial pit; hungry, like a mouth cavity looking for offerings.

Whoever opened the door was luring Adam to step inside. He quickly realized that the room was no longer his; it had become a home for something else. Something which had been herding him here, through the call on his cellphone.

Like prey standing right before the predator's lair, for a few seconds he froze, trying to calculate his chance of survival. Then he stuck his head through the door, entering the dark vacuum.

He only wanted to make sure of what had been waiting for him inside, but at once a nauseating odor raided his nostrils, jolting him back into the hotel corridor. He panted for air, as if the few seconds in the room had drained his whole energy.

He was ready to run away from the cursed place, but the Earth seemed to have given way beneath him. Then, a powerful force pulled him, sending him diving, head first, into the room. The door behind him swung gently to a close, as light as a hand's wave, without any help from the wind. It chased away all the light from the room, isolating him inside.

A gust of musty, putrid wind blew into his face. The sickening smell crawled up his nose, choking him, making him yelp, like a hunted animal caught in a trap. His throat felt like it had been thrusted with a rod, forcing him to spill out his guts.

He tried to calm himself down and steady his breathing. He tried to observe every inch of the room around him, but he could not see a thing; it was as if he had been made blind. He couldn't find where the ceiling ended and the ground started; everything seemed endless, as if he was floating in a time before the universe was created.

The sudden sound of air being inhaled deeply hit his eardrums, startling him. The sound did not come from his own windpipe but from someone, or something, else, hidden in the dark with him. Something in the sound made him shudder. He narrowed his eyes strenuously, hoping to see anything which would explain where the sound had come from, but the blackness around him had no inclination, it seemed, to give him what he asked for.

He heard the breathing again, this time louder, as if whoever it was were trying to suck every milligram of oxygen from the air.

He crawled backward, toward the unknown. He felt that the source of the sound was now closer than before. His own breathing sounded puffy. He turned his head around quickly, trying to fathom the geography of the room which confined him, looking for a way out. When the cursed sound was heard once again, he crawled on his hands and knees, like an insect trying to run desperately from a bug spray.

The breathing now sounded so near that he felt he could touch it. So greedy, as if air was the only thing which could quench its thirst. So loud that its sharp whistle could maybe tear one's eardrums.

As he was crawling, he felt all four limbs landing in something wet. The sound of water, splashing as it came into contact with his palms, made him suspect that he was in the part of the hotel room that he knew the most well. He knew that he was right, because a speck of light, seemingly coming from nowhere, enabled him to see the flooded bathroom floor. The plastic bottle for his sedatives was still there, empty and forgotten, no longer possessing its magical powers.

Still moving away from what was ahead of him, his back found a ceramic-tiled surface. Icy cold, it gave him goosebumps. Even before turning his head, he knew what was waiting for him there: the bathtub, which had now become a coffin for his wife-to-be. From the darkness, he could see the water in the tub creating ripple after ripple, as if whatever hid beneath was giddy with excitement at finding him.

He gasped as the surface of the murky water suddenly grew turbulent, bubbled and parted. Something dark arose, slowly breaking the water, like a goddess ascending from the bottom of the Earth, its hair wet and coiled like a snake; its eyes wide with an eternal wrath; its face black, rotting away, encroached by bacteria.

He could hear its heartbreaking gasp for air—he knew the sound well, because it was the last thing he had heard coming out of Gita's mouth before the water flooded her lungs, finally making her stop writhing. Even now, in her death, she longed for air.

The water creature reached out its cold and squishy hands for Adam's face, cupped it and pulled it closer, as if trying to make the man himself step into the bathtub. And he did not fight it. He felt extremely tired; all he wanted was sleep.

The wrinkly hands of the undead slowly lowered Adam's head into the water and held it there until no more bubbles were coming out of his mouth.

He had finally got what he wanted: he was free from human mockery, back in his lover's arms; laid to rest in the same coffin.

Who's there, awake with his eyes shut?
Who's there, howling above the echoes?
Did you know the wrath that I call home?
In there, your eyes will be opened; your wish will be granted.
Silence all of your praises.
Let me uncover the lies of the universe.
Kneel down before my altar,
So I can whisper things in your ears tonight.

AT DUSK

The tiny house, just seventy meters square, stood on a neglected, barren yard. The colonial-style building was deeply rooted to the ground, its back against the cloudy afternoon sky. Its walls revealed the scars and wisdom of surviving all kinds of weather, much like an ageing human.

I adjusted the position of my backpack before taking a deep breath and walking toward the building. Beads of sweat started to trickle down my forehead, although the temperature outside was supposed to be its lowest at this time of year. It seemed like my nerves had been acting up without me knowing. I tried to remind myself that was a normal reaction.

This was the first time I had been sent on a field duty by the editor of my high school magazine. The assignment was to interview a celebrity—a mystery novel writer, whose literary work outsold the get-rich-quick guidebooks, teen-lit paperbacks and self-improvement books. With such an achievement, my editor-in-chief had thought the hotshot worthy of an article.

I took another deep breath before pressing the doorbell, which emitted its two familiar notes. It didn't take long before the wooden door in front of me opened to reveal an old man. I suspected that he was around sixty-five years old; wearing a gray T-shirt, he looked at me with his melancholy eyes.

I immediately greeted him and introduced myself as a representative from the school magazine, which had recently contacted him. He nodded and invited me in.

He offered a long, carved wood bench for me to sit on in the dim, chandelier-lit living room. His courtesy extended to serving drinks and snacks, to fuel our conversation. He prepared these himself; no family members were in sight.

The old man kindly asked if I had driven here, and if the house had been hard to find. I answered that I had come by public transportation, and that it was easy to find his address. I then asked if he lived here with his family, regretting it as soon as the question had left my mouth: *What if he no longer has a family? What if he thinks the question intrusive?*

Thankfully, his expression didn't change a bit. He explained that his family did not live in the city, but came to visit once in a while. In return, he often went on a railway trip to see them.

I felt that the ice was breaking quite quickly after that. He asked me if I planned to study journalism in university. I replied truthfully that I was interested in a lot of things, and did not want to limit myself to one particular field; still, journalism was something which I was currently into. The man complimented the flexibility of my mindset, and I thanked him.

Our chit-chat went on for about ten minutes, before I felt it was time to lead our conversation toward the main subject. I launched into the questions I had written and rewritten in my notebook.

As my ears heard the interview flowing out of my mouth, I realized how lazy and cliché-ridden were the questions I thought I had prepared so well. "Where does your inspiration come from? Who is your favorite writer? What message do you want to convey to young people who aspire to be like you?" Ultimately and consequently, the answers he gave were no different from the anonymous jargon found aplenty on the internet. Still, I admired the old man for treating my mediocre questions seriously, as if doing a T.V. interview session. As he elaborated his replies, I continued to nod and take notes.

It was as I was scribbling in the pages of my notebook, that I heard a tune softly coming out of his mouth: a repetitive, rhythmic melody, typical of children's songs from an older time. I couldn't quite catch all of the lyrics, but the rhyme was similar to *pantun*[1]:

"Last night, the moon dimly lit,
Dusk creeping in, fingers reaching out,
Shadows overcast, eyes wide open..."

The old man came to a halt, as he realized that I was watching him. I saw him take a deep breath, before asking me if I knew the song. I spontaneously shook my head. He laughed and said, "It's a song the parents of olden days used to sing, to call their children back home, so they don't wander around at *Magrib*[2]."

---

[1] A Malay poetic form, usually consisting of a quatrain, with an *a-b-a-b* rhyme scheme.
[2] The time for sunset prayer, one of the five obligatory daily prayers performed by Muslims.

I listened, nodding occasionally. I looked at the gray sky painted behind the window; it was indeed close to dusk. I was still mesmerized by the shades of the gray clouds, when once again I heard laughter coming from the old man sitting next to me. I automatically turned to him, and the man amusingly explained that he would always be scared when his mother started to sing the song at dusk. I couldn't help but smile.

"Why?" I asked.

"My mother said the song could summon *Kelinting*, the spirit dweller of the woods, who often kidnaps children and sucks their blood when it is time for sunset prayer. Whenever the song was heard, children would race home in terror," he replied.

I listened to his tale with a smile. "Do you believe the story?" I asked.

He looked back at me tentatively, before replying, "I didn't… at first."

"At first?" I repeated.

The man took his time to respond. For a few seconds, he only looked at me, reluctance reflected in his eyes. Then, he broke the silence with a sigh, asking me to promise that I would not publish in the magazine the story he was about to tell me. "Your editor-in-chief wouldn't be happy," he joked. Sensing a good one coming, I gave him my word, before he proceeded with his story.

"A long time ago, when I wasn't even ten years old, I lived with my mother and father in a village called Probongkoro. The place was so remote that the only school was a small madrasah[3], *owned by a Quran tutor we called Pak Suro. Every day, from noon until after-*

[3] A type of educational institution which emphasizes the study of Islamic religion.

noon, he taught the children how to read, count and recite the Quran. Not many children went to school there, since the location was not easy to get to; the children had to walk or ride their bicycles through the woods, to get there—a distance of about ten kilometers!

"But, for us who studied there, going to school through the woods with our friends was quite an exciting experience. And, for me, it was much better than having to help my father in the rice field. The residents of the village thought highly of Pak Suro; he always gave reassuring advice and encouragement. He taught the children patiently, even when we were naughty and unruly.

"One day, Pak Suro told us he was planning to hold a pesantren[4] *program at the school. Children who were interested in participating had to spend three nights at school, for Quran recitation skill refinement and intensive prayer. Outside the program, he would keep teaching the children to read and count.*

"I wasn't interested in this pesantren program because, as exciting as it was to explore the woods with my friends every morning and afternoon, spending three nights in it must be extremely boring and, if I could be honest, terrifying. But, my parents forced me to join—'So that when you grow up later, you will be an exemplary man,' my father reasoned with me.

"So, I went and stayed at Pak Suro's pesantren, but I secretly made a pact with one of my friends to run away on the second night. We planned to meet behind the school after Magrib, to get away quietly, before it got darker. When the day came, I hurriedly walked to the meeting point, right after sunset prayer, for our

---

[4] An Islamic boarding school.

rendezvous. At first, I thought he wasn't there, because all I could see was the rubber trees.

"But, then I saw him: he was sat behind one of the trees. He was covering his face with his hands, crying. I didn't understand what could have possibly made him cry like that until I realized: my friend and I were not alone in the woods.

"My eyes caught something hiding behind the trees, waiting for the sun to set, its eyes wide open and glaring wildly, as it looked for the child with the freshest blood to be devoured. When its eyes locked on mine, I felt my heart stop beating. I didn't get a chance to process what was happening, because right then and there I broke into a run—and I kept running into the woods, leaving my friend behind. I just sped up, not wanting to stop, because I knew that whatever it was that had scared my friend was now pursuing me.

"The hunter's voice reverberated in the orange sky, calling at me to come back—roaring repeatedly, its voice hoarse, ancient and echoing. I ran faster and screamed louder than anything else in the woods, as I realized what it was that was chasing me: Kelinting, the blood-sucking creature my mother had told me of. The children in the village, including I, knew him as Pak Suro."

The old man finished his story with shaky breath, and a face as white as the wall—I was quite surprised to see the effect of this story on the man; he looked truly scared.

I ventured to ask if the story was some of his new material because, if it was, I loved it; I was a huge fan of ghost stories.

He rolled his eyes toward me. "Then, you will like the end of this story."

"How does it end?" I asked.

The man replied, in a voice so deep that it sounded like a growl:

"I didn't survive that night."

When he said that, I saw the smile on his face—a smile that I had never before seen on any human being. His lips cracked open, wide like that of a snake, revealing rows of yellowed teeth sticking out of his red, swollen gums.

Coming from that ear-to-ear grin was the now-familiar song:

"Last night, the moon dimly lit,
Dusk creeping in, fingers reaching out,
Shadows overcast, eyes wide open,
Kelinting came; all hair stood up.
Kelinting came; all hair stood up.
Kelinting came; all hair stood up..."

THE WANDERING

Who wouldn't be curious about time?
Everybody wishes they could jump into the future or the past at any time,
Reliving their youth and delaying their golden days, just like a dream.
Or is there a way to outsmart Death's cunning scheme?
Why don't you write something... or two?
Across time throw all your bliss and blue,
With a chisel or a pen, whichever will carve deepest.
Then, you'll be truly timeless, like an eternally roaming ghost.

Badrun was held spellbound by the magical verses engraved on the book in his hand, when a squeak broke the silence of the office building he was patrolling that night. His body jerked back a few inches; his left leg, which was crossed over his right and crudely stretched out on the reception desk, almost knocked over a two-way radio, standing upright next to him. As it turned out, the source of the shrill, megaphone-like sound in those wee hours was the black, plastic transceiver.

"This is Azis from the first floor, for Badrun from the seventh floor. Over."

Upon hearing his name, Badrun hastily reached for his radio. He brought it closer to his mouth, pressed the small, protruding button on the top of the device and started talking.

"Go for Badrun. Over," he responded, then lifted his thumb, releasing the button to its jutting position.

The skinny twenty-eight-year-old had been working as a security guard in this building for six months, and he still wasn't familiar with communicating through the radio. He peered at the black device with its long antenna, cradled in the palm of his hand, and waited for a response.

A buzz, distorted by distance and air, crept out of the loudspeaker embedded in the device. His ears just caught the voice saying *"Are there any people left on the seventh floor? Over."*

Badrun replied that a lone member staff from the accounting department was still working in a cubicle in the left wing, but she usually left by eight p.m. "I'm sure she will leave soon, Bang[5]," he explained. "Over."

From the first floor, Bang Azis—a middle-aged man, who was the central communications commander—reminded him to turn off the lights in the right wing, to which he promptly replied, "Copy that. I did it already, Bang." He had switched off of all the lights in the right wing of the seventh floor—the topmost floor of the low-rise building—after making sure that no one was there, working overtime.

Bang Azis went on to remind him to turn off all of the lights in the left wing, after everyone had gone home. *"But, before you do that, make sure that there*

---

[5] Short from "Abang" (big brother); a form of address toward older men, to show respect.

are no valuables left in the cubicles. If you see anything like that, lock it in the receptionist's drawer."

"Roger that, Bang," Badrun replied, swiftly.

"We don't want people thinking that we take their things. The missing promotional gifts and petty cash on your floor and the fifth last week are still being investigated, so we have to be alert; let's prove to them that we can be trusted." Bang Azis continued.

Bang Azis was known to have a no-nonsense personality and took the sanctity of his mandate seriously—and he was insistent that all team members who patrolled with him every night adopted the same attitude. Badrun had heard a story, from his fellow security guards, about the time Bang Azis had severely reprimanded a team member—an absent-minded young man named Rohim, who was caught leaving his assigned post to take a coffee break in the drivers' canteen, in the basement—until his whole body was shaking like a bobble-head cat figurine.

"Who's working overtime there?" Bang Azis asked.

"Mbak[6] Annisa, from accounting," answered Badrun. At her name, his mind conjured up an image of the 25-year-old woman, who looked more mature than her age. Her hair was dyed orange, making her look like a *bule*[7], in his eyes; her voluptuous body was wrapped in a tight, white shirt; her bosom full and firm—he couldn't help but steal a glance at her.

---

[6] A Javanese prefix used to address older sisters or other women of unknown age, to show respect.

[7] A commonly used word in Indonesia to describe foreigners, especially Caucasians.

"She's sexy, isn't she, Bang?" Badrun uttered, amidst his fantasy.

Bang Azis's voice immediately scolded him, sounding sharp, as if his tongue was made of a plastic sheet. *"Hey, remember your pregnant wife at home!"*

Badrun chuckled and argued that admiring God's creation is not a sin—though, he was sure he couldn't crack a cheeky joke like that in the presence of Ningsih, in her seventh month of pregnancy, who waited patiently for him to come home to their small, rented tenement unit every night. Bang Azis and his other colleagues in this office didn't know that Badrun had yet to marry Ningsih, despite their having been together for nearly two years. He had saved enough to pay for a wedding officiant at the K.U.A.[8], but alas Ningsih had got pregnant before they got around to it. The twenty-year-old, who had left her hometown to try her luck in the capital city, asked Badrun to marry her at the K.U.A., as previously planned, but he was now adamant that he also wanted to hold a modest wedding celebration. It had now been five months since he told Ningsih to be a little more patient, because he had gotten a job as a security guard for, in Badrun's words, a big company. But in reality, even with the money from this "big company", he still could not afford the celebration he dreamed of. Most of his wages went toward the regular pregnancy check-ups, with a midwife at the community health center, various vitamins and newborn this-and-that—the latter of which, luckily, were available in abundance at the nearby morning market.

---

[8] Kantor Urusan Agama (Office of Religious Affairs).

Badrun and Ningsih had yet to discover the gender of their baby, but the expectant mother had a feeling that it would be a boy. So, now and again, they bought stuff for a baby boy. But, what if her prediction was wrong?

"Well, even better," his young partner once said to him, jokingly, "because she will grow up a tough woman; she'll see right through womanizers like you."

Bang Azis's voice, coming from the black device in his hand, suddenly interrupted his daydream. *"Such a dirty mind you have, Drun,"* his superior said.

Badrun laughed, heartily. "Boys will be boys, Bang," he justified, humorously. As his laughter subsided, he heard Bang Azis telling him that the elevator on the left side of the corridor was temporarily out of service—he needed to tell his colleague because nobody had put a sign on the elevator doors, to warn people about the technical glitch. The Human Resources department had explained that technicians from the elevator company could not come before the following day to fix it. It appeared that occupational Health and Safety was not a priority in this office.

Badrun confirmed the message and ended the conversation, after his supervisor said to him, *"Over and out,"* just like he was in some television show.

Badrun put the radio transceiver back onto its stand, which also functioned as a charger, and was about to resume his reading, when he heard a female voice from the left-wing office.

From the corner of his eye, he could see the woman—Annisa—walking toward where he was sitting. She seemed to be talking to someone, but he couldn't see who it was. As she got closer, Badrun realized that the woman was on the phone.

"The name of the building is Graha Sugi, Pak[9]; right next to a mini-market," she said, giving directions to—Badrun assumed—the driver of a taxi she had ordered. After a while, she said into her phone, "Kaveling[10] Fifty-Nine, okay? No, not Berkat Street, Pak; the street-name is Adiwarna. I'll be here, waiting."

Annisa ended her conversation with the driver, as she stood by the closed glass door, facing the corridor where the two elevators were. She was still looking down at the screen of her expensive, sophisticated cellphone, her face illuminated by soft light emanating from the sweeping and tapping of her fingers.

Maybe she's sending a text to her boyfriend, Badrun thought, as he scanned Annisa's body with his eyes and his libidinous mind. He pondered how lucky was the man who got to make out with Annisa: her porcelain skin, her curvy body, her clothes and other luxurious attributes—all which radiated high social status—and her slightly bitchy expression; all of those killer ingredients which brought his fantasy into being: a woman out of his league, whom he could never touch, let alone fondle.

In his heart, he often complained about how Ningsih, the woman who would soon become the mother of his baby, was too meek and obedient; she never resisted his lustful desires. But he knew to keep this whinge to himself, and not to let it spill out of his mouth: if Ningsih knew what he really thought of her, the woman would be utterly devastated. He might be a womanizer, but he didn't have the heart to hurt Ningsih. And, while

---

[9] Short for "Bapak", a prefix used to address a fatherly figure.
[10] A designated plot of land.

he might not always let her know it, in truth, he felt helpless when he was away from her.

Still, despite all of that, and to help fill the emptiness the night, he boldly launched his opening gambit with the woman standing before him.

"Did you order a taxi?"

Annisa looked up at him and nodded. He asked her why she didn't just hail one directly outside the office, where taxis are usually standing by. She explained that she wasn't sure if there were still any taxis outside at this hour.

"Is the driver familiar with the area?" Badrun asked, to continue the conversation.

"I'm not sure," replied Annisa, with a slightly grumpy expression that he liked. "The driver keeps asking, 'It's on Berkat Street, right?' when I've already told him, over and over, that the street name is Adiwarna, not Berkat."

Badrun responded to her annoyance with laughter. He jokingly suggested that she cancel her order and find another taxi driver. The woman was hesitant to do this, though, out of pity for the driver. "From his voice, I can tell he's an older man," said Annisa.

Badrun ventured himself into risky territory. "That might be even more dangerous, Mbak. Why don't you ask your boyfriend to pick you up?"

This time, the laughter which came out of the woman's pressed lips sounded like a two-syllable grumble, and it was pretty easy to tell that she was now no longer interested in continuing the conversation. But Badrun, never one able to read between the lines, persisted. "On a Friday night, like this, wouldn't it be better to spend the night with your boyfriend than with a taxi driver?" His mischievous laughter tickled the air.

Annisa shot him a stern look, and it was only then that he shut his mouth. Her knifelike stare made him expect a spicy retort, but then the woman simply re-dialed the driver's number, stuck the phone to her ear, and started talking, whilst walking toward the door. "Hello? Where are you, Pak?" When the access card she held close to the door was replied by a high-pitched, polyphonic ring, she was able to push the door and step outside into the corridor. After she left the lobby, the glass door behind her swung shut, giving her temporary protection from Badrun's thirsty eyes.

Annisa was still talking on her phone when he saw her push the button which called the elevator on the left side of the corridor. As she waited for the doors to open, he could tell that she knew she was within range of Badrun's vision—like a zebra in the savanna, being staked-out by a predator; he enjoyed the view from where he was sitting behind the wooden desk.

A wave of fresh energy surged over him every time he saw other people growing anxious by his presence. In these moments, he felt like he had some kind of inner power, which could force people to tremble before him.

Badrun kept watching Annisa, who seemed more and more restless, as the elevator took forever to arrive. A voice inside told him to help the woman, who clearly couldn't wait to go home, but another voice, much more cheerful and inviting, kept persuading him to watch his female prey a little longer. He pursed his lips into a smile, stretching the skin around it like a filthy sheet of paper; grubby and grimy.

"What are you looking at?" the woman finally snapped, spontaneously activating Badrun's self-defense mechanism, to save its host from fear and embarrassment.

"I just wanted to let you know, Mbak, that the elevator on the left is out of order. Use the right one, instead," he explained, half-shouting from behind the closed glass doors, so she could hear him clearly. He pointed to the functioning elevator for good measure.

Annisa did not retract her reprimand, though, keeping her annoyed expression, as she turned around to follow Badrun's direction, facing the elevator on the right-hand side of the corridor.

He saw the elevator doors slide open, not long after her finger had pressed the button with the downward-facing arrow, and the woman stepped into the carriage, which gave off a pale glow from the inside, like the light of a refrigerator. After the two stainless steel doors slid shut, confining Annisa, the carriage unit took her down to the lobby on the ground floor.

Immediately, Badrun felt an intoxicating sensation which, for the last six months, had been stinging his nerves like a colony of fire ants; pumping adrenaline all over his body and making his senses more sensitive and alert. All because he knew that every time the last member of staff left for home at night, he became the ruler of the floor.

It gave him an immediate authority to check every desk, peek inside every drawer and get a taste of every expensive item left by its owner—all in the name of office security. He had lost count of how many employees' belongings his hands had groped, from a camera worth tens of millions, to compact loudspeakers, cutting edge headsets, a buttery-soft leather chair, which customarily seated an executive, and a variety of food and drink in the office pantry, the likes of which errand staff and security guards could only dream of.

The young guard stood up from his chair behind the reception desk, fastened the radio to the belt around his waist, then walked down the corridor, toward the left wing of the office, from where Annisa had just left. The sound of his soles, tapping on the nylon layer covering the floor, became the only sign of life in the entire office area.

His company every night was just rows of desks and cubicles—like him, left by their masters. All documents, personal belongings, and leftovers recklessly abandoned on their desktops were expected to still be in place in the morning. Surely it wasn't the masters' fault if their documents were accidentally thrown away by the errand staff, who had the initiative to clean up the work area. *"It's not the errand staff's place to throw away documents they don't even understand,"* they would rant. But don't blame the masters when their desks are as chaotic as the metropolitan's urban planning system, either. *"It's the errand staff's job to clean our desks before we arrive."*

And, don't even think of accusing the masters when luxurious items, left behind at the office of their own volition, were never to be seen again: they would lament, report and demand, as if the world had no right to tarnish their dignity in such a way. *"Why do the errand staff and security guards steal? Is it not enough that we give them holiday bonuses and disbursements every year? If they still need money, all they need do is ask nicely and we will give it to them, wholeheartedly,"* they would say.

Badrun felt that it wasn't fair he and his fellow security guards were accused of stealing from the office, especially when the owners left their belongings lying around invitingly on the desks, tempting the faith of those who only wanted to get a taste of something new. Though he *had* taken some stuff and money during his nightly patrols of the office, he didn't think he was to blame.

At first, he only took trivial items, like stationery: a daily planner and a desk calendar. But then his craving fingers started to explore various goodies designated for company events, like shopping vouchers and faux-leather wallets. One night, his wife-to-be, who was suddenly showered with all kinds of new stuff, asked him where he had got them. Badrun lied and said that the office was feeling generous, giving away all of their leftover promotional gifts to security staff, as a token of appreciation. Ningsih, who never questioned anything he said, never asked again after that. In his eyes, she seemed happy with the goodies he brought home, especially the shopping vouchers.

Other office stuff, which they had no use for, turned out to be a good source of income when sold to the neighbors. A small amount of extra money managed to flow into their savings, which would later be used for the baby's necessities.

Then, a few weeks ago, Ningsih had told him that she was hemorrhaging. After being examined at the community health center, the midwife suggested that Ningsih be taken to a referral hospital. The midwife suspected that there was an infection in her uterus, but she couldn't tell for sure, since the health center didn't have an appropriate scanner to detect the problem. So, worried for the safety of his wife-to-be and the baby, Badrun had taken Ningsih to the referral hospital, where ultrasound imaging had confirmed the midwife's suspicion: there were abnormal growths in her uterine wall called polyps which, if left untreated, according to the doctor, could mutate into cancer. But the doctor assured Badrun that the condition was curable, as long as she took the prescribed medicine and came back regularly for follow-up visits.

The figure written on the hospital bill gave him a stomach-ache. He realized that the fund they had been saving for the baby would be drained for Ningsih's medical expenses. To make matters worse, he and Ningsih could not use the subsidized health facilities provided by the government, because neither of them had any insurance or social security. Even if they wanted to sign up, they had to arrange for identification cards first, something which they had never bothered to have. Ever since that day, his head had been filled with wild, ferocious numbers, which pounced on him from the stacking bills. Every night, the sharp-cornered sheets of paper seemed to nibble on the kapok in the mattress he slept on with Ningsih—gnawing on it, little by little, until the razor-sharp teeth reached their toes, biting them off inch by inch, starting from the soft outermost skin to the savory layer of flesh, deeper and deeper every time, until nothing was left but a series of bones, curling up in terror amongst the kapok flakes.

Badrun knew that he needed money fast, and he knew how to get it. Each department on every floor had a petty cash pot, kept by the division secretary in the cabinet of their workstation, which was usually locked. But the skinny guard was never short of wits; he had managed to take the spare keys from the control room on the first floor, when he had visited Bang Azis's station one night. Every night after that, no matter which floor he was stationed on, he would manage to snitch a few notes, which he found folded and crumpled in a glass jar. For quite a while, the theft went unnoticed by the staff and security guards. But gradually some of the workers started to realize that the balance of their division's petty cash did not match the books.

At first, as usual, the secretary trusted with the fund was accused of stealing. But, after all of the secretaries subsequently reported similar phenomena, showing their books to prove that they had never embezzled a dime, the management instructed the personnel and facilities departments to carry out an investigation, focused on the days when the thefts had allegedly happened. Facilities also urged Bang Azis, as head of the building's security, to tighten up on all floors, a command which was relayed to his subordinates.

Unafraid of the ongoing investigation, and with a confidence parallel to that of a criminal who always managed to get away, Badrun walked without any loss of composure, toward the cabinet in the secretary's cubicle, where his ultimate reward awaited. His body swayed as lightly as his gait, passing the empty interdepartmental mailbox, the small fire extinguisher, and the wall calendar with the company's logo, which showed today's date as Friday, March 30, 2001.

When he reached the secretary's work area in the left wing, he knelt down on the carpet. Faced by a pink, plastic-framed hand mirror, which hung on the cabinet door, he could see his own reflection there. His pupils glowed eagerly, like the eyes of a rodent who had just found food crumbs on the floor. His sparse mustache hung below his nostrils, obscuring lips which looked like they were stifling a laugh. From his pocket, he took out a set of keys, fastened to an acrylic keyring.

Each key had its mate embedded in the cabinet of each secretary in the building; he knew by heart which key fitted into the hole in front of him. His fingers skillfully inserted one of the keys into the hole in the cabinet door, turning it sideways, until there was a click—the loudest sound he had heard since the elevator doors closed and caged Annisa earlier that night. Badrun opened the plywood door of the cabinet, eager to get his hands on his main target.

A cracking sound from nearby made him immediately shut the cabinet door and turn around. He quickly stood up from his kneeling position in front of the cabinet, to avoid suspicion, should there happen to be another member of staff, or a security guard, coming round to inspect the floor. He shot his gaze over to the seventh-floor lobby, from where he suspected the sound had come.

Before him was a long corridor, flanked by desks and cubicles on each side, giving way to the carpet spread toward the lobby, and the right-wing area, which was no longer bright. Badrun strained his ears, trying to catch the slightest sound which would signal the presence of another human being on this floor. He couldn't hear anything.

Again, he knelt down in front of his treasure chest, opened the wooden door and saw the three compartments, full of stacks of paper, stationery, rows of plastic folders and Post-its, in their many colors and sizes. But the prize he hunted wasn't there.

He frowned. He was sure he had seen a 9-inch glass jar with an aluminum lid, stuffed full of folded notes and coins, greeting his hungry eyes every time he opened the cabinet door, on many nights before. But this time there were only useless things inside; it looked as if all of the paper and stationery in the cabinet had been deliberately lined up to spit at him, with laughter and mockery. *Where's your money now, thief?* they mocked.

Badrun thought on his feet. *Of course the secretaries won't keep the money in the same place as before—not after the recurring thefts of the past few weeks.*

The young man hoped that the notes and coins he sought were being kept somewhere he could guess; he didn't want to waste his energy rummaging through every cabinet and drawer on the floor. He didn't want to leave any more traces, which could be easily sniffed out by the amateur sleuths. And, most of all, he didn't want to come home empty-handed. The lives of his child and wife-to-be depended on what he could bring home tonight.

Badrun opened the doors to the larger cabinets, in the secretary's work area, hoping that the diversion method she had deployed had been so naïve and stupid that he could easily find the jar containing hundreds of thousands of rupiah, inside the first cabinet he opened. But his coveted treasure was still reluctant to show itself; for the umpteenth time, he saw only stacks of stationery, none of which could ever fill his family's stomachs.

Badrun sighed, as if he was already exhausted, before even turning all of the cabinets inside out. The image of Ningsih lying on the sofa, watching T.V., along with their baby inside her tummy, swirled inside his head like a cloud. He knew that his wife-to-be was waiting for him to come home every night, hoping that he had received a bonus, incentive or other appreciation, such as he boasted to her every time he stepped inside the house. He knew that only the green, worshipped by so many, could buy the safety of his wife-to-be and child. He knew that the monotonous days he had spent in this building for the last six months would only feel meaningful as long as he could bring home something which would make her eyes shine with pride. The amber inside his heart slowly started to reignite.

He was building up his courage to check every nook and cranny of every cabinet, desk, and drawer on this floor, when a rattling sound pierced the silence once more. It sounded like the thud of a wooden object hitting the wall. His heart skipped a beat.

Assuming that there was someone visiting his floor, Badrun quickly stood up and began walking toward the seventh-floor lobby, his post for the night. While making his way there, he called out to the person he thought had just entered the room. "Bang Azis?"

He didn't hear any reply, and when he reached the lobby, he knew why: there was no Bang Azis there. In fact, the room, designated the first to welcome guests, looked empty underneath the dim lighting. The reception desk, from where he had ogled Annisa on her way home an hour ago, looked exactly how he had left it. The anthology he secretly liked was still lying open on the desk, its pages kissing the wooden surface.

He was still observing every inch of the room surrounding him—the lobby imprisoned by silence; the halls alienated from the hubbub; the walls neglected by the cacophony—when a peculiar shriek burst the air.

His body stiffened with shock.

It was only a few seconds later that he realized the high-pitched scream, which almost tore his eardrums and stopped his heart, was none other than the sound of the distorted radio waves coming from the communication device on his belt. As if from another universe, a voice distorted by the layers of concrete comprising this building called out to him.

"This is Azis, from the first floor, for Badrun on the seventh floor. Over."

Badrun snatched the device free from his belt, pressed the talk button and responded to his supervisor's call. "This is Badrun from the seventh floor, for Bang Azis. Over."

He heard Bang Azis asking for an update on his floor, and replied that Annisa, the accounting staff, had gone home about an hour ago, and that he was now patrolling the floor. His supervisor reminded him not to touch or remove anything from the staff's desks; he did not want his team to be accused of making a mess or looting their stuff. Badrun concurred with the supervisor's command.

He then remembered the noise he had heard. His eyes drifted to the empty hall where the two elevators stood, facing one another. Right outside the stainless steel-framed, glass door, locked by the electronic access system, there were two small corridors, each facing the right and left wings; from where he was standing, the view to the ends of the two corridors was blocked by the walls enveloping the lobby. He could still recall the loud thud which made him come to the seventh-floor verandah less than two minutes ago. To shoo away his curiosity, he asked, "Are you still on the first floor? Over."

The head of security gave him an affirmative response, and another name crossed the younger man's mind. "How about Rohim, Bang? Is he still on the third floor?"

Once again, the supervisor replied with a yes, and added that all of tonight's team members were at their respective posts. *"Why do you ask, 'Drun? Over."*

At first, Badrun was hesitant to explain, but he finally caved in. "I thought there was someone on my floor, Bang. I just heard the sound of a door closing."

As he released his thumb from the talk button, he heard Bang Azis's laughter in response to his revelation. *"Come on, Badrun, this is not your first night. Those noises are heard every night by every security guard in the building."*

Badrun explained that for the six months he had been working in this building, he had never heard anything so out of the ordinary.

"Are you sure you're not sleeping on the job every night?" Bang Azis quickly retorted. This was followed by more laughter. *"Then, it's good that you've never heard anything: it means you'd never been* pestered,*"* said Bang Azis, after his laughter subsided.

Badrun asked his supervisor what he meant by "pestered", although he could guess where the conversation might lead.

Starting to patrol from the control room, on the ground floor of the building, the middle-aged man explained that the office buildings along this street were known for their "inhabitants". Badrun immediately asked what his supervisor meant by "inhabitants", though he knew exactly the meaning within the context of this conversation—he just wanted to hear the head of security say it.

"Well, of course it means ghosts, 'Drun. Goblins. Demons..." Bang Azis then went on the name all of the identities he could think of, by which the magical

creatures who aroused the curiosity of so many usually went.

He then told stories of security staff who had encountered strange happenings on their night shifts in the building. There was one who, patrolling the fifth floor one night, swore that he heard the clickety-click of a keyboard, as if human fingers were typing on it, when the clock clearly showed it was almost midnight—and, according to this storyteller, there was no one on the floor except for him. There was another, who found that all of the cabinet doors and drawers were wide open, despite being locked and tightly shut just a moment earlier. A few had reported computers and photocopiers turning themselves on and operating like they had a mind of their own, after being checked that they were switched off, while many witnessed the elevator doors opening and closing on their floor, without anyone having pressed the button.

Badrun tried to respond to his supervisor's stories in a lighthearted manner. "Why would goblins or demons bother turning on a computer? Or typing, or opening cabinet doors? Are they employees of the company?"

"Well, of course they do it to scare us, 'Drun," Bang Azis replied, a little impatiently, as if his analysis was an empirical fact, which should have been believed without question. He then elaborated his opinion that the inhabitants also needed somewhere to live; "*We already use every room of this building from morning until evening; from dusk until dawn, it's their shift."*

Listening to his supervisor's convincing voice, Badrun couldn't help but laugh. The head of security, who was still pressing the talk button, didn't know about the mocking of his subordinate, and went on and on with his theory:

"It's like living in a house-share with others, 'Drun: when we take something of theirs, they reprimand us."

Badrun disagreed with his supervisor's notion. In his opinion, none of the night security team ever meant to disturb or violate anyone's rights. When they stayed up all night, fighting off drowsiness and exhaustion in this building, they were only doing their job, the best they could to earn a living.

Again, Badrun heard the head of security chuckling. *"It means the inhabitants here are basically mischievous,"* concluded Bang Azis, as if the topic they had been discussing in the last few minutes was now worthy of a conclusion.

Before they ended the conversation, Bang Azis's last comment made Badrun shudder, echoing in the alleyways of his ears. *"They're exactly like us, 'Drun. There must be some amongst them who like to scare others."*

The sparsely mustached young man put his radio transceiver back into its charging cradle on the reception desk, after Bang Azis signed off, reminding him to keep alert. Trying to put the conversation from his mind, Badrun reached again for his book on the desk, looking for a quick way to wash away the trivial information in his head, with strands of sentences which made him feel safe and calm.

But, before his fingers were able to lift the book from the wooden surface, something which hadn't been there before caught his eye. As he moved the book away, it revealed a sealed envelope underneath—

Badrun swore the envelope wasn't there when he was reading a few hours ago.

The supposedly white letter wrapper looked yellowed, as if time had contaminated every fiber in it. On the front side, he could see for whom the letter inside was intended, the black ink on the paper displaying a name and an address:

Zakaria Suwardi
Jalan Berkat No. XI
Central Jakarta, 10570.

Badrun turned the paper envelope around in his hand so that he could see the triangular flap, which was no longer sticking down the back of the envelope. Just like a little boy who came upon a plate of snacks on the table, with no signs of the rightful owner, his hand intuitively reached into the mouth of the envelope and took out the content inside. As he suspected, the envelope contained a letter.

Badrun sat down on his chair and unfolded the newly discovered sheet of paper, stretching it out before him. Unconsciously, a smile spread on his face; secretly spying on other people's privacy had always been exhilarating for him. The pounding in his chest made him feel like when he was twelve, snooping on the girl next door taking a bath. The longer he could stay uncaught, the more curious and addicted he became. The handwriting filling up the page in front of him now ignited the same curiosity.

The young man began to read.

Karangwetan, May 20, 1999.

Mas[11] *Jaka,*

I hope you're already in Jakarta by the time you receive this letter. I pray that Gusti[12] *Allah will always protect you. I hope your trip was smooth and enjoyable.*

What is it like in Jakarta, Mas? Is it as impressive as the images we see on television? I heard from some friends who have been there that buildings in Jakarta are taller than coconut trees. The streets are wide, solid and smooth. They say that, even at night, the lamps in the buildings and the streets continue to shine so brightly they make you forget that it is already late. Ah, if only I didn't have to help Ibu[13] *with her business every day, I would go there with you. But I understand that you must take care of Pakde*[14] *Kus until he recovers, especially after Bude*[15] *passed away.*

Poor Pakde. Even though I've never met him, I know you've been close to him since you were little. I will always pray for his recovery, so that he can be healthy like before, and is able to come to our wedding.

Speaking of weddings, my father has spoken with Ustad[16] *Ali, who is willing to wed us in the mosque,*

---

[11] A Javanese prefix used to address older brothers or other men of unknown age to show respect.
[12] A Javanese word, which means "God" and is used as a prefix to His name, "Allah".
[13] "Mother" in Indonesian.
[14] From "Bapak Gede" (Javanese, literally means "big father"), which refers to an uncle older than one's parent.
[15] From "Ibu Gede" (Javanese, literally means "big mother"), which refers to an aunt older than one's parent, or the wife of Pakde.
[16] Honorific title for an Islamic scholar.

free of charge! Alhamdulillah[17]*... I cannot thank Gusti Allah enough for blessing me with such wonderful parents, friends and husband-to-be, along with beautiful dreams that will soon come true.*

I apologize if I sound too mellow, Mas. It's just that my heart cannot contain this happiness. I can't stop myself from smiling while writing this letter. I hope you find joy reading my silliness.

Oh well, I don't want to take too much of your time with a long letter. Write back to me when you have time. Ibu and Bapak[18] *at home asked me to send their regards to you.*

Please take care of yourself, Mas. Send my regards to Pakde Kus and everyone there. Also, please send me pictures. I want to see your face. And, I want to see Pakde, his house, and how Jakarta looks.

Sending you a long, big hug.

Rahma.

After he finished reading the handwritten letter, Badrun swept the page with his eyes, from top to bottom, flipping the paper over as though to make sure he hadn't missed any. Again, he examined the top-left part of the letter, which showed the place and date that the love memoir was written; his eyes reread the words lining up there: *Karangwetan, May 20, 1999*. The name

[17] An Arabic phrase meaning "Praise be to God".
[18] "Father" in Indonesian.

of the location did not ring any bells in his head. But the date, month and year lining up behind it told him that the letter he had just read couldn't be older than two years. The one thing which sparked his curiosity most was the fact that there were still human beings who communicated by pen and paper—he actually liked the idea.

But his affection for older communication methods couldn't tell him from where the letter had appeared. Badrun surely didn't remember seeing an envelope lying on the desk, when he was sitting in the reception area earlier that evening. He knew by heart every item on the desk he was stationed at, night after night: one radio transceiver unit; a book to kill time; an electronic access card, attached to a lanyard, to be hung around his neck; a company desk calendar, which never moved from its place; and a cup of black coffee to keep him awake all night… A letter from somebody who was madly in love is not something he would leave lying around at his post. And, even after working here for six months, he didn't know anyone by the names of Zakaria Suwardi or Jaka. He was filled with questions.

How is it possible that this letter suddenly appeared here? Could it be that somebody has been up to this floor without my knowledge? He recalled the strange noises he had heard a few minutes ago, and he knew that Bang Azis had already assured him that every member of security staff was at their respective post. Could it be that someone other than the security guards had infiltrated his floor? Could it be one of the office staff returning to prank him with the letter?

The young man was still deep in thought when another loud crack could suddenly be heard, breaking through his ears.

His body jolted, as if electrocuted. He dropped the ownerless piece of paper onto the desk and turned his head in the direction of the sound. This time, the noise, which sounded like it was born out of silence, seemed to be coming from the left-wing corridor, where he had just been ransacking for money.

Badrun walked over to the left wing, deliberately thumping the floor harder and faster with each step—giving off an impression, he hoped, which would threaten whoever was messing around on his shift. The closer he drew to the work area, filled with its cubicles and computers, the faster he walked, not wanting the intruder to get away. A moment before stepping onto the work floor of a hundred square meters, he loudly called out, "Hey, who's there?"

His call was immediately replied by the silence. Even as he arrived at the work area, with its rows of empty cubicles, he knew that there was nobody there but himself. The intruder he hunted seemed to have disappeared into thin air.

His eyeballs swept across the deserted view before him, circling the rows of desks. A dozen monitors protruded from their surfaces, like tombstones in a graveyard: mute, silent and dead. The lamps hanging from the ceiling in long glass tubes were switched off, emphasizing the vibe that shadows were lurking everywhere. Badrun pressed down all of the light switches on the wall-panel beside him, sending the troops of light to slay their shadowy enemies. As soon as his eyes adjusted to the blinding light, he moved, combing every cubicle and every room, assuring himself that there was nobody hiding in them.

He was just about to move to the next row of cubicles when something odd caught his eye. A sixty-centimeter filing cabinet, hunkered down below the desk he was just about to pass, was hanging wide open, revealing its contents.

Badrun knew for sure that all the cabinets paired with the desks were always left with their doors closed; some were even locked in response to the recent thefts in the office (caused by none other than himself). But the wooden cabinet in front of him, which caged all of the usual folders, documents and stationery, was now standing with its door wide open, revealing what had been hidden inside.

Badrun knelt down on the carpet, examining the open cabinet up close. From the folders and documents stacked inside, he knew whose work area he was in: the cubicle belonged to Annisa, the accounting woman who had earlier filled his head with lustful desires; the blonde with the bitchy face and tantalizing curves, who had snapped at him an hour ago, in front of the elevator.

Badrun peeked inside the cabinet and found something tubular, hidden behind a row of books and documents—from its silhouette, Badrun could easily deduce the identity of the object he saw, deep in the corner of the cabinet. The guard enthusiastically reached into the cubic space before him, bringing out the glass jar he had been looking for, filled with bank-notes.

All of the strange happenings of the last hour now forgotten, he screwed the aluminum lid open and scooped out the notes and coins onto the carpet. A contented smile spread on his greedy face, as he realized just how much money was scattered on the floor before him: from his calculation, the cash must have been worth around two million rupiahs—more than enough to cover Ningsih's medical expenses for the next few months.

But Badrun knew that if he did not want his activities to be easily detected, he could only take a small amount of the money; he would wait for the right time to rob the company's other departments, once assigned to another floor. He inserted a couple of notes into his wallet and put the greed-quenching glass jar back into the cabinet after stuffing it with the remaining notes and coins.

He was just about to close the cabinet door and stand up when he saw something: an object similar to that which he had found a while earlier. Once again, an envelope was in front of him. It was lying on the shelf, where the glass jar was kept.

At first, Badrun thought that it was just an office document, filed there by Annisa, who owned this cubicle. But, when his eyes caught the inked etching on the surface of the paper, he knew that it was the same type of letter he had found a few minutes earlier. Curiosity triggered him to reach for the envelope.

The surface was bumpy and stiff, as if it had been exposed to splashes of water before being left to dry under the sun a long time ago. The previously white paper was now stained with marks which could only be left by time. The same name and address as before were written on the front cover:

Zakaria Suwardi
Jalan Berkat No. XI
Central Jakarta, 10570.

He took the folded piece of paper from the envelope and spread it out; rows and rows of the neat scratching of black ink filled his view. From the date printed at the top left of the paper, he could surmise that the letter in his hand was written a few months after the one he had read earlier. Most people would probably ignore aged verses, clearly addressed to people they didn't know, but for a daydream-addict like Badrun, reading, watching and listening to stories about other people's lives always managed to arouse his curiosity. So, he began to read:

Karangwetan, November 28, 1999.

Mas Jaka,

I'm so happy to receive your reply. I was worried something had happened on your way back to Jakarta. In the six months I was waiting for your letter, I couldn't think of anything else. Ibu and Bapak always told me never to stop praying to the Almighty, because only Gusti Allah is able to give protection wherever His servants go. Thank God for your letter. I was so relieved, especially when I saw the pictures you enclosed. You look healthy and happy in Jakarta. I couldn't help but feel happy when I saw you smiling widely in the picture. Is the man sitting in the middle of the sofa Pakde Kus? He's older than I thought.

I'm sorry for being impatient to wait for your reply. I forgot that you must be so busy. It must be exhausting taking care of an invalid without any help from other family members, especially if they can no longer walk, like Pakde Kus. Oh, I just remembered that you told me Pakde Kus lived alone in his house after his wife passed away a year ago. Who's the woman sitting next to

Pakde Kus, Mas? She looks so pretty. Is she one of Pakde's nieces? If she is, then you're lucky to have somebody to help you, giving you time to reply to my letter. I'm kidding, you can write me when you have time—I don't want to burden you.

Mas Jaka, Bapak already told Ustad Ali to book the function hall of the mosque in February next year for our wedding. I pray for Pakde's recovery by then, so that we can get married soon. If you still need to go back to Jakarta to take care of him after the wedding, it's fine. I can go along with you as your lawfully wedded wife. Ah, just thinking about it makes me smile like a schoolgirl. If you could see me right now, you would burst into laughter, Mas.

I'd better end this letter. I hope it doesn't take you long to reply. It never took me more than a day to reply to yours. Ah, once again, please forgive your impatient wife-to-be. My mother always says that when I want something, nothing can stand in my way. She told me to recite Quran more diligently to calm my nerves. She said any husband would hope for an obedient wife that was not demanding, so that their household would always be peaceful and long lasting. I promise I will keep learning to be a suitable woman to you, Mas. My heart belongs to you and only you. And I also pray that no matter how far you go, and no matter how pretty the women you encounter there, your heart belongs only to me.

I enclosed this picture to show you how much I miss you. So that every time you miss me, you can take a look and hold me, so I can feel it too.

Longing for you,

Rahma.

Badrun reached inside the envelope, where he found the picture mentioned in the letter: the passport-sized photograph, now lying in his palm, showed the face of a girl not more than nineteen years old, smiling modestly back at Badrun. Her long, black hair was twisted in a braid, her body wrapped in a red, long-sleeved blouse, which made her stand out amongst the other elements in the picture. A long, black skirt hung from her waist to her ankles and her feet—clad in a pair of simple mules—were grounded to the soil, which looked wet. Her slender body was standing before a house painted light green, with a window on its right side. Based on the information gathered from the writing, and from the photo before him, Badrun concluded that Rahma was a woman who had not only been born and raised somewhere far from the city, but had also not been exposed to modern women's fashion and style of speech which, in his opinion, could sound arrogant and conceited. After reading everything the woman had poured into her letter, he felt like he knew her. *She looks like Ningsih*, concluded Badrun.

The face of his wife-to-be glowed in his heart, as if she were imprinted on his retinas. Both women were simple, modest and soft-spoken, but he realized that Ningsih had something more than most women: behind her mildness, the woman carrying his baby was adept at manipulating his heart. He might misbehave when he was away from home, but he had never once had an affair with another woman since meeting Ningsih. She was always able to make him grant any wish, without having to whine and beg for sympathy. He imagined that if Ningsih had been in Rahma's shoes, she would have been able to persuade her husband-to-be to come home and obey her request without an ounce of pressure.

Thinking about Ningsih made him want to run home to her, but he knew that his shift would be over in just one more hour—ten p.m. to be exact—when his colleague Agus would arrive in the building to continue his patrol round. Besides, Badrun quickly dismissed the urge to ask his superior for early dismissal, because he didn't think Bang Azis would let him.

He decided to walk back to the seventh-floor reception desk, to unwind and read his book, to kill the remaining time. After returning the letter to the cabinet, he closed its wooden door, hanging open, and locked it.

The moment he stood up and turned around, he saw something which made him feel that his heart chamber was choking on its own blood.

A shabby envelope, just like the one which had appeared before him a few minutes ago, was on the floor, front side up, as though it had been delivered by invisible hands. He automatically stepped back, away from the envelope, as if the rectangular piece of paper would wriggle to life and leap at him.

From where he was standing, he could already see for certain that the letter lying before him was a part of the same correspondence series. The envelope, which was surely filled with more words of longing, was still addressed to Jalan Berkat No. XI in Jakarta, to a young man named Zakaria Suwardi, and written by a woman named Rahma.

"Damn it!" he spat his curse word into the air surrounding him. Fright started to crawl over his skin, compelling him to run away from where he was. But arrogance tightened its grip on his instinct and forced him to flaunt his valor. "Who's there? You sure have plenty of time on your hands! Show yourself, you son of a bitch!" he shouted.

The only moving object now inside the boundary, set by the soulless walls, was himself. He froze, his eyes sharp and alert, as he swept the alcoves and corners of the room. Everything he saw inside the office showed no signs of change or movement; the rows of desks divided by the cubicle walls were still vacant; the seats of the chairs accompanying them were still filled with air; the electrical technology on each desk was still asleep, not at all bothered by the sounds of his roaming footsteps and heavy breathing.

He decided to swallow his pride and head back over to the lobby, where his radio transceiver was being charged. Badrun was dying to contact Bang Azis—not only for company to kill the time, but also to tell of everything that had happened to him in the past hour. He knew that Bang Azis might at first bark at him for being a coward, but he didn't care: at least a reprimand would occupy his senses with sounds from the mouth of a human he knew, rather than tricks from some imaginary hand. He was just about to start walking when he realized something: the envelope lying on the carpet, about a meter from him, now appeared different.

As if some magic charm, the thing had managed to turn itself over, without the help of any human hand; the envelope before him was now lying backside up. Badrun could see the triangular flap of the envelope wide open, revealing the emptiness inside.

Before his mind could even question the whereabouts of the envelope's content, the skin covering his fingers sent a signal to his central nervous system…

The letter that was supposed to be inside the envelope was spread open in his hands.

As if licked by flaming coals, he flapped his hands, trying to fling the two sheets of paper to the floor, but they stuck to his palm. Like leeches, the sheets of paper glued themselves to his fingertips, unwilling to let him go. With his free hand, he pulled at the letter, which felt embroidered onto his skin. He felt as if stung by a bee whenever he struggled to free himself from the supposedly lifeless piece of paper. As he raised his hands, he could see redness seeping into the fibers of the paper: apparently, his efforts had torn his epidermis, as evidenced by the fresh, gaping wound underneath the ripped layer of skin on his fingertips.

Sweat crept out of the pores on his face. His cussing words could no longer give him courage. Whatever he tried to do could not bring him any closer to being free from the letter, which was laden with words of yearning. So, his logic told him that the only thing he could do was read the letter which clung to his hand.

He forced his eyes to look at the rows of handwriting, which had by now become familiar to him, and began to read:

Karangwetan, February 17, 2000.

Mas Jaka,

Thank you for your letter, Mas. I was so happy to hear news from you quicker than before, knowing that you are busy taking care of Pakde Kus. Now it is me who is taking a long time to write a reply. Please forgive me. In this letter I will explain why I didn't write to you for so long.

But first, my mother, my father and I would like to extend our sympathy to you for your Pakde's condition. It's hard to believe that there are no doctors in Jakarta who can cure him. I thought Jakarta is where the smart people are. How about bringing him to Karangwetan, Mas? Maybe he'll feel better from breathing the fresh air and meeting all the people here. It's calmer and cooler in the village than in the city—maybe it can lend him the will to live. I can also help you take care of him, so you won't be too exhausted. But I leave the decision in your hands. You know what's best for him. Please take my suggestion into consideration.

Mas Jaka, it's now February. If you read my last letter, you will know that by this month and week, we would have gotten married. But I understand that you need to stay there for Pakde Kus, especially because you told me his condition is deteriorating. I keep praying for God to give His miracle and take away the sickness. I also pray that we both can soon see each other and proceed with our marriage. I hope we still share that same dream, Mas.

Mas Jaka, like I said earlier, there's a reason why I didn't get to write to you sooner. Actually, I have been sick for the past two months. About two weeks after I wrote my last letter, I got a high fever. Ibu and Bapak told me that my whole body was so hot, although honestly I felt like I was freezing until my nails turned blue. My lips were sore and ulcerous, making it hard for me to eat and drink. Ibu said it was just a symptom accompanying the fever and it would go away once I drank a lot of warm water, ginger tea and jamu[19] *that she made. After I drank all of those regularly, the fever broke. But every night I had a strange dream. Oh, Mas, if only I could write down the things I dreamed about every night, but I can't. I won't even try to remember them. I can only do* dzikir[20] *every night before bed, praying that those dreams won't visit me again as I close my eyes. But every night the dreams came to me and I found myself screaming when I woke up. I felt so guilty toward my mother and father. I could see the panic and confusion in their eyes when they saw the state I was in. They scrambled to my bedroom every time I woke up with a scream. Every time they asked me what I saw in my dream, but I just couldn't tell them. But, one thing I can tell you, Mas, is that in my dreams there were always you and me, and... something else. Something vicious and violent, which seemed to be lurking in my sleep at night. Ah, just thinking about it gives me goosebumps. Thank God the dreams are over.*

But then I really didn't want to sleep anymore, no matter how exhausted I felt and how heavy my eyelids were. After almost a week of no sleep, Ibu and Bapak called a registered nurse to examine me. He gave me a medication that supposedly made me fall asleep. He promised that, with his medicine, I would sleep a dreamless sleep. At first, I said no. But, honestly, I was really exhausted and I just wanted to rest. After I asked

---

[19] A traditional medicine drink made of herbs and other natural ingredients, mostly found in Java.

[20] A devotional act in Islam, in which prayers are recited repeatedly.

the nurse to promise me that I would no longer be haunted by those nightmares, I took the medication.

In the beginning, I didn't think it worked, because I stayed awake all night, staring at Bapak and Ibu, who accompanied me in my bedroom. I told them that the medicine given by the nurse was not potent enough. "Maybe it's not that the medicine is not potent enough, but that you're forcing yourself to stay awake. Don't be afraid, Bapak and Ibu are here for you. Close your eyes, my child. We will always be here for you," Bapak said to me. I remember that at the time I felt like crying, because I knew he was right: I was afraid to fall asleep. I was so scared that those nightmares would come and make me see those wicked things. It didn't help that rain started pouring out of the blue, with terrifying thunders and all. I felt like the universe was telling me something bad was going to happen. But I always believed Bapak and Ibu would protect me, even when I was asleep. So, after a while, I squeezed both their hands, closed my eyes and tried to get some sleep.

It was unbelievable, Mas. I slept like a baby and didn't dream a thing! Or maybe the dreams came, but I couldn't remember them. It felt like all my fears were gone with my consciousness. For a while, I felt relieved and at peace. But, apparently, something strange happened while I was sleeping. When I woke up the next day, I saw Mother holding my hand. Her eyes looked like she had been crying all night. When she realized that I was awake, she called Bapak. They both hugged me tightly and stroked my face, as if I had just got home from a very long journey. When I asked them why, at first they tried to dodge my question. They told me, "It's nothing", but I didn't believe them. It couldn't have been nothing if my mother was crying like that. After threatening that I wouldn't take the medicine again unless they told me what had really happened, Bapak told me that I did something strange when I was sleeping that night. At first, I didn't understand what he meant by that. If I had been sleeping like he said, how could I have done anything? Bapak told me that at first he and Ibu thought that I was sleeping. They took turns staying with me all night, ensuring that I slept well and would not be bothered by those nightmares. And, according to them, I did sleep well until past midnight. They didn't see signs of me growing restless or delirious, even though the weather out there was at its worst. The rain had been drenching the village for the past hour and showed no signs of stopping. At around two in the morning, the rain petered out and Bapak asked for my mother's permission to do his night prayer in their bedroom, since all his prayer gear was there. Ibu, seeing that I was fast asleep, granted her permission and was willing to stay with me by herself for a few minutes.

Poor Ibu. It seemed like she was so exhausted that she admitted she fell asleep not long after Bapak left her for his prayer. She woke up when my father tapped her shoulder in panic, asking her where I was. Ibu told him that I was still asleep on the mattress, but when she turned to see, I was no longer there. Bapak told me that they were calling my name and went looking for me everywhere, inside and outside the house, but they couldn't find me. They were terrified. It was dark. The roads around the house, if you still remember, have no lighting whatsoever, and our nearest neighbor lives hundreds of meters away from us. Realizing that they couldn't ask anybody for any help, Bapak ran outside carrying an oil lamp, calling my name in the middle of the night, while Ibu continued to pray for my safety on the front porch. Bapak almost gave up when he couldn't find me, but in the midst of his exhaustion, he saw footprints on the wet soil. Bapak inspected them closer with the light from the oil lamp, and they were footprints of a human, barefoot, with toes and all, going farther away from where he was standing.

Believing that they were my footprints, Bapak ran along the trail until he heard the sound of water. When he walked closer to the source of the sound, he could see the fast-flowing river, which was nicknamed Sungai[21] *Gugah by the locals, for the thunderous sound of its current was said to be able to awaken any creature which fell asleep there. Bapak once told me that a lot of children went missing, carried by the strong current, when they were playing and swimming in the river. Thinking that I too had fallen down there, Bapak ran to the riverbank, calling my name amidst the rolling current, until his voice became hoarse. He looked around frantically and finally saw someone standing at the edge of the river, not too far from where he was kneeling. Imagine his relief when he saw that somebody was me, still wearing the same clothes I was in when I went to sleep, standing with both arms hovering above the jutting rocks, as if getting ready to jump into the river. According to him, my eyes were shut at the time,*

---

[21] River.

my face expressionless, as if my soul was not inside my body.

He called my name repeatedly, grabbed my shoulders, and tried to wake me up. He told me that I finally opened my eyes, but I wasn't aware of where I was. I asked him what he was doing there, what that place was, what we were doing there. When I saw him baffled by my questions, I broke down and cried. You might never know how it feels, Mas, knowing that your body is not under your control. As if the movements of these hands and feet were controlled by a puppet master, and not yourself. I remember asking: Oh God, what kind of disease have you brought upon me? What should I do to be free from this malady? What would have happened to me if Bapak had not found me on the riverbank that night? *I would probably have left this world and could no longer write to you, Mas.*

After that incident, Bapak invited Ustad Ali and his students to pray for me. My soul was at peace listening to the saintly boys chanting the prayers. Ustad Ali was also very kind. He came every evening before Magrib, voluntarily, and sincerely recited the holy verses with me. After the prayers, according to Bapak and Ibu, I slept like a baby. I no longer sleepwalked or did anything strange in my sleep. I no longer had nightmares. All by the power of The Almighty, with the help of Ustad Ali. I don't know if I will ever be able to return his kindness, other than pray that God grant him good health, happiness and prosperity.

I apologize for only telling you this now. I really don't want to make you worried. I know you always have to take care of your Pakde until he recovers. But, thinking about what has happened to me in the last two months, and thinking about you spending all your energy and attention to take care of your sick Pakde, I realize that our time in this world is in the hands of Gusti Allah. I don't want to wait any longer to be with you. I miss you too much.

Can I join you in Jakarta, Mas? I have discussed this with Bapak and Ibu, and they give me their permission as long as you promise to be with me and protect me. Once I get there, I promise I will help you take care of Pakde Kus, clean up his house and cook for both of you, so that you don't get sick too. I hope you also think this is a good idea, Mas.

Is the woman in the picture the one who's been helping you all this time? I thought she was one of Pakde Kus's nieces, but you said that she's his neighbor, isn't she? Like I said, once I'm there, let me be the one to help you, Mas. It must be a burden for this lady to have to take care of other people's family. But please send my regards to her. You mentioned her name in the previous letter, but I forgot... Oh, it was Ningsih, wasn't it? Please say hi to her for me.

Ah, look. I have written you pages and pages of letter. I'd better stop. I don't want you to get tired reading about my troubles. Please consider my request to join you in Jakarta, Mas.

Missing you always,

Rahma.

Badrun felt his hair stand up on end. He reread the last two paragraphs of the letter. He couldn't believe that Ningsih's name was written in it.

He wondered if whoever wrote this letter knew Ningsih, or if she was talking about another woman with the same name? His eyes followed the rows and rows of writing in the letter, starting from the first line. An address was written there: *Jalan Berkat No. XI.*

He quickly concluded that the letter had not been addressed to this office: the building he was in was located on a street called Adiwarna, not Jalan Berkat. He didn't even know the location of the street written in the letter. Although it had almost been two years since he left his hometown to live in the capital city, it was still hard for him to remember all the corners, nooks and alleys of Jakarta, especially since Ningsih didn't like him roaming around and leaving her at home. "What if you meet some other woman out there and don't want to come back home?" Ningsih always said, in her adorable, sheepish way.

Then, he realized something; the address written in the letter suddenly sounded familiar to him. He remembered hearing the street's name mentioned by Annisa—whose feminine curves he was crazy about—not too long before she went home with a grumpy face.

"Not Berkat Street, Pak," Badrun remembered she had said to the taxi driver about to fetch her; "the street name is Adiwarna."

As his eardrums delivered the past exchange to the innermost cavities of his hearing organs, an assumption was slowly building in his mind. Badrun asked himself: *What if the two street names refer to the same location? It isn't uncommon for street and neighborhood names to change. What if these horrible letters have always been addressed to this building?*

But to whom? There's no one in this building named Zakaria Suwardi. And, if there was, why must I be the one reading them?

The questions came to a dead end, as if there was something preventing him from seeing the answers. His head felt like it was spinning; the ceiling, floor and everything in between were swinging wildly, as if blown by the wind.

With the pages of the letter still glued to his hand, he tried to grab anything firm enough to maintain his balance. But his fingers could only grasp air. His wobbly body staggered backward, followed by his two feet, which were frantically looking for something by which to anchor themselves. The walls surrounding the room became the first, which he could finally lean his back against. His nose and mouth gasped for air, to bring him back to consciousness, but the view before his eyes remained the same: spinning, as if every element of the Earth wanted to keep him from seeing the real world.

His thoughts were filled with images of Ningsih, his wife-to-be waiting for him at home. He wanted to go home. Her voice and embrace always made him feel protected from terrible things; her way of talking and her gentle gaze always managed to clear his head whenever he was troubled; her caressing fingers on his head always made him forget everything. Ningsih really had something that most women didn't. She always had, since the first time their eyes met nearly two years ago, at a bus terminal in Jakarta.

He was just about to walk toward the lobby, feeling his way along the wall with his hand, as if his eyes could no longer see, when he noticed something.

Another piece of paper, as shabby looking as the ones before, appeared on the surface of the wall, right underneath his spread hand—it didn't take a moment for him to realize that the worn-out sheet of paper was not the letter he had read a few minutes ago. The new piece, which also now felt like it was embroidered to his hand, was the next letter in the series of heart-spill, by a woman named Rahma, from Karangwetan.

Honestly, Badrun didn't want to read a thing from that letter. His body and mind were now wrapped in one desire: to come home to Ningsih. Thoughts of her were circling around his head, like a spirit roaming the air, luring him to come home. But the young man felt another force attempting to smother his and Ningsih's desires—something as powerful, as persistent, but awash with vengeance and anger. He couldn't help but reach for the piece of paper sticking to the wall, pull it closer to his face, and begin to read:

Karangwetan, April 1, 2000.

Den[22] *Jaka,*

I hope this letter finds you at the correct address. I copied it from the letters Rahma wrote to you. I hope it doesn't take long for you to receive this. I am writing to you now because I want to tell you something.

Den Jaka, my wife and I are deeply saddened. Our only daughter, Nur Rahmawati, whom we loved very much, has passed away. She has probably told you herself

---

[22] Short for the Javanese word "raden", used to address a younger male.

about her health condition in her letters. For the last two months, she couldn't leave her bed. Her entire body was hot from the high fever and she was always restless in her sleep. Every night she woke up crying. When my wife or I asked her why, she always said she dreamed that you would never come back to her, because there was another woman in your heart, but the woman did not have good intentions. My wife and I tirelessly tried to calm her down, but she kept on crying every night. We believe our daughter missed you so much that she carried that yearning to sleep, which then became her nightmares, and fell ill because of them. We asked her to keep her correspondence with you to ease her longing. But her condition never got better. One night, we even found that she had nearly jumped into the river. If I hadn't found her, she might have left us sooner. My wife and I were worried that her longing for you made her desperate. Since we didn't know what else to do, we asked Ustad Ali to give her advice and guidance. Ustad Ali told us that Rahma was sad because your marriage couldn't proceed as planned. She was also sad that you took such a long time to reply to her letter. She felt like you had forgotten her.

Ustad Ali tried to console her. He told Rahma to follow the example of the wife of Rasulullah SAW[23]*, Siti Khadijah, who was incredibly patient, even in circumstances which could be seen by women as trials. Ustad Ali asked her if she wanted to be like Siti Khadijah, who was known not only for her beauty, but also for her*

[23] One of the many appellations of the Islamic prophet, Muhammad SAW, meaning the "Messenger of Allah".

beautiful heart, because that's the kind of woman who will always lead her loved one home. Her heart seemed to soften after listening to Ustad Ali's words of wisdom. For the next few days, her fever seemed to subside and she could sleep better. She no longer woke up in the middle of the night because of the nightmares.

But two nights ago, around subuh[24]*, after my wife and I finished our morning prayer, my wife went into her room to wake her up. I heard my wife shout her name, and I immediately went to my daughter's bedroom and saw that her bed was empty. She wasn't in her room, but we saw that her bedroom windows were open. My initial thought was that she had sleepwalked outside, just like before. I ran outside calling her name, but I didn't hear her reply. Somehow, I knew she went to Sungai Gugah, just like before. My guess was right: there were footprints going that way. Fortunately, it had rained the night before; the soil was wet and footprints were left where someone had stepped on it. When I got to the riverbank, I couldn't find her anywhere. All I could see and hear was empty land and the loud gush of the current. I kept on calling my daughter's name, but she was not there.*

We reported the incident to the head of our village and he gathered the young men of the village to search for Rahma. Ustad Ali and I also went looking with them, while the women held a mass prayer in the mosque with my wife. Evening came, but we were nowhere nearer to finding her, although it felt like we had looked for her

---

[24] Dawn or daybreak. Also time for the Islamic morning prayer.

along the riverbank, in all the lands and houses of all of the villagers, and in the woods bordering the village. We asked around, but no one claimed to have seen Rahma since dawn. It was as if she had vanished into thin air, or was swallowed by the earth.

But, around Magrib, when we were getting ready to do our sunset mass prayer at the nearest musala[25], *we heard the news. Someone claimed to have found the woman we and the villagers had been looking for, but the person didn't say any more and asked all of us to come, so we could identify her ourselves. Thankfully, the owner of the* musala *kindly gave me a ride on his motorbike to the location described by the person, and when I got there, I met the young man who claimed to have found Rahma. I couldn't thank him enough and started asking him questions about her condition.* Was she hurt? Did she tell him where she had been since dawn? Where was she now? *The young man seemed unable to respond to my questions. He told me that maybe it would be best if I saw her myself.*

He brought me to the riverbank, not fifty meters from where we had met. I could see the spread of wet soil around the river and rows of rubber trees, which were planted to keep the water from overflowing. Under one of those rubber trees, my daughter sat with her back leaning against it—I could recognize her at once from the red blouse she was wearing. I hurriedly came over to her. She was sitting there with her eyes closed, like she was asleep. I shook her and called her name, but

---

[25] Prayer hall.

she didn't reply. The young man accompanying me confirmed my biggest fear. Rahma was already dead when he found her, her body having been dragged by the current, to the rocks surrounding the river. The young man had carried her body out of the water before the current took her farther away. I held my daughter's body, begging for Gusti Allah to bring her back to life. But, deep inside, I knew that my daughter was gone.

With the help of the village youths, I took Rahma home. When my wife saw her, she could only cry. But I knew we had to be strong, so that her soul could find peace in Heaven. Rahma was buried two days ago. I apologize that I didn't write to you sooner. I hope you understand.

Den Jaka, my wife and I don't want you to feel guilty about her departure. We know that you are very busy taking care of your sick relative in Jakarta, and going back to Karangwetan from Jakarta costs a lot of money. We only ask you to forgive our daughter for all of her wrongdoings and pray for her soul to find peace in the hereafter. Our daughter loved you very much, even until her last breath. I found a photo of you together in the pocket of the blouse she was wearing when she died. I also found traces of your letter to her, but unfortunately it was torn apart after being immersed in the water. Thankfully, I managed to salvage a picture of the two of you from the letter, and I'm enclosing it here for you. Rahma looked so happy in this picture. I hope you remember her this way.

I'll end this letter here. I hope that Gusti Allah always protects you. If you're ever in Karangwetan, do visit us. You've always been like a son to me and my wife. I hope we can meet again.

Wagiman.

Badrun's gaze shifted to a stiff and crinkled piece of a photo. Whatever shape and color would have been captured in it had been flushed by water, but the man could still make out the two people standing side by side in the picture. The woman, whose face he recognized from the photo enclosed in the earlier letter, was again present in this one, but there was something different in her expression: her smile was no longer sheepish, but spread so wide that you could not see her eyes anymore. To him, she looked very happy.

Beside her was a dark-skinned man who was also smiling, albeit vaguely, as if his happiness was ousted by something much more powerful: a dream? An ambition to reach something more? He was very familiar with the face, because it was the face that looked back at him every time he stood in front of a mirror. It was his own face, smiling from the worn picture, standing side by side with a woman named Rahma—a woman who, he had only just realized, was someone he had known for a long time.

His head was now spinning, turning the world upside down through his optic nerves. The more he tried to pick up the traces of memory scattered inside his brain, the more jumbled the Earth and the sky, as if something in the universe was furiously trying to keep him from remembering.

The longer it went on, the more positive he became that he had known Rahma for a long time. Slowly, he recalled a piece of memory: her serving him drinks and snacks every time he visited her house. How she had smiled shyly when her father teased her in front of him. How she had looked to the ground sheepishly when he held her hand and took her out to the night market at the village square. He remembered the red blouse and sarong she often wore, because she loved the striking color. And the tears which rolled down her face, when he looked into her eyes for the last time, before boarding the bus which would take him to the city.

How could I forget her? Badrun wondered. *How could all of my senses erase her without a trace from my memory?*

Again, something inside his mind attacked him like a snake, trying to keep him from remembering. His entire body was fixed on a mandate, the way it always happened, whenever his mind drew a few inches closer to the truth: to go home to Ningsih. Ningsih, who was expecting their child. Ningsih, who had offered to help him take care of Pakde Kus, during their first conversation in the bus terminal, two years ago. Ningsih, who didn't mind being impregnated by a reckless man like himself.

The woman who could always turn him into a submissive, and get him to do whatever she wanted, without his feeling like he had to. The woman who, with her charm, could make him forget not only his lover back in the village, but also his uncle, whom he had left to die in a pile of his own feces. He had even forgotten the name his parents had given him since birth—to the point where "Jaka" became no more than an ownerless nickname. A beauty who was able to manipulate him without being despicable. The charmer, who whispered her magic words into his ears, so he would stay by her side in the concrete jungle, even though he was not brimming with fortune.

"Ningsih..." his tongue, silenced by the tight grip of the charmer, defenselessly whispered its master's name.

"Rahma..." his mouth cavity was finally able to echo the name of his lover in the village, exactly one year after her demise.

Two forces fighting for his body and soul.

He hurriedly walked, his fingers running along the walls like a lowly reptile, trying to protect himself from the raging wrath of the two women. His nerves had long since given up on him, and he hadn't even noticed that the power suddenly went off, blinding him with endless black corridors.

He dragged his lame feet toward the exit. He knew there was a side door nearby, which would take him to the outer corridor, toward the elevators, and his tactile senses found a corner of the wall, which he knew would lead him to a stainless steel-framed, glass door; he let the corner lead his footsteps.

He was mere steps away from the gate which would grant his freedom, when a faint whisper called to him:

"Mas Jaka..."

After such a long time, Badrun spontaneously turned upon hearing his birth name called out.

And, for the first time since two years had passed, he heard the woman's voice again—the voice he had neglected on the seabed of his past.

Even in death, Rahma kept her promise: she really had come to Jakarta for him—but now only her vengeance remained.

From the corner of his eye, he saw a flash of red in the midst of the pitch-black room, standing three meters away from him. And, when the dark room was betrayed by the light, he could see anger plastered on Rahma's face.

The woman's eyes were so white, they seemed to scream out at him from the midst of the blackness. Her hair, no longer braided, spilled out in an unkempt cascade all the way down to her ankles. Except for her soaking wet, all-red attire, the figure standing before him resembled in no way the modest woman smiling at him from the picture. All of her past demeanor had been peeled away, revealing a face which seemed to have nurtured only a grudge from beyond the grave.

He stepped back toward the exit door, which was suddenly behind him, to stop him from crashing through it. The heavy steel wouldn't budge, even when he pushed it with the weight of his body. He quickly remembered that all in-and-out passages in this office could only be opened with electronic access cards, which had to be scanned by the card reader, protruding on the right side of each door. He had left his card on the seventh-floor reception desk, along with his radio transceiver, dozens of meters away from where he was at this moment.

He knew there was no way he could get away from Rahma, but still he kept trying to push the door open, to no avail. He was now no different to a rat, trying to free itself from a trap which had it pinned down by its tail; he knew how it felt to be the prey. His paranoia and hysteria defied all logic; he wanted only to be free from the wrath of the siren.

His screams filled the air when the woman's figure moved toward him. Her movements were smooth, as if her feet were floating on water. Her arms stretched forward, eager to squash her lover's heart.

Badrun punched the door with his fist, repeatedly calling for help from anyone who could hear him. When the darkness failed to lend a hand, he knelt down and begged the floating woman in red.

He clasped his hands above his bowed head, as if offering his worship and prayer. His apology bounced back from every corner of the room, as if it had just been rejected by the ruler of the heavens. He started to roar like an animal, his cognition gone. Tears and mucus from his nose filled his open mouth, drowning his tongue in bitterness.

Badrun's unintelligible cry pierced the air when Rahma's ghost floated closer to him. He could see her rotten fingertips, curved into sets of claws, ready to ram them into his fleshy, sweaty skin.

Desperate, he frantically punched the door behind him. His roars for mercy, and the thundering sounds of steel and glass being pounded, seemed to be replying to each other. Anyone downstairs should have heard the ruckus, but the air seemed to be conspiring with Rahma to keep any sound from escaping. For the first time in a long time, Badrun said a prayer.

His doom, disguised in the form of a woman, was now floating in front of him, staring at him without an ounce of mercy. He closed his eyes, waiting for the cold hands to grip him at any moment.

He heard a familiar, high-pitched sound, and he opened his eyes. A *crack* came suddenly from the door behind him, and at once he understood the meaning of the sound. He pushed the door one last time and, surprisingly, it swung open, as if giving him a second chance.

Not wasting the small miracle given to him, whoever it was from, the young man ran out of the room, toward the long, unlit corridor. He turned his head to the right, as the steel door he had just passed through closed behind him.

But, hunting him, the woman in red had also come out into the long, dark corridor, her arms reaching out, her eyes glaring wildly.

Badrun ran to the left, where the two elevators were located. He pressed the down button several times, desperately trying to summon the metal carriage, which would bring him to the safety of the ground floor. The doors to the left-side elevator took forever to open, and he could see from the corner of his eye that the woman in red was closing in on him. For the first time, he could see her smile—a sign that she would win. He pushed the button for the umpteenth time and, right at the last moment, he heard the chime he had been hoping for.

The metal doors before him slid open, inviting him to step inside; his heart leapt with joy. He stepped forward, thinking that his foot would be welcomed by the floor of the carriage, which would lead him away from the Grim Reaper.

But the safety he longed for refused to embrace him. That the left-side elevator was out of order briefly crossed his mind, just a moment too late. Why the elevator doors had opened for him, he would never know.

His body plummeted into the hollow space, where the metal cube which hung from the steel pulley was supposed to be. In those last few seconds, he knew that, even in her death, Rahma would not stain her fingers with his blood; the woman wanted him to kill himself. Finally, it was her time to get what she wanted.

When his free-falling body hit the roof of the dormant carriage on the ground floor, it looked like the Earth had just gifted Rahma her favorite color.

THE VOICE CANAL

The autumn wind was still blowing softly that morning onto Gio's face. He was lying face down on his keyboard when he heard a knock on the door. Struggling to open his eyes, he heard a voice calling him.

"Gio? Are you awake?"

Gio took his time to reply. He blinked a few times and stretched out his arms and shoulders, stiff from supporting his head all night. It was only when the voice outside called his name again, and knocked for the umpteenth time, that he responded.

He walked over to open his front door and found Anggi, who lived in their shared flat, with a look he immediately recognized as a plea for help. At twenty-five, the woman was the same age as him.

"Yo, sorry to wake you up this early. Have you had any problems with your internet connection since yesterday?" asked Anggi.

"No, I chatted for hours last night," replied Gio.

"I also wanted to chat with my mom, but the internet kept failing to connect. Can you help me out?"

Gio took a deep breath, fighting his drowsiness as he walked toward Anggi's room, a mere five steps from his own. Anggi watched as he sat down in her chair and started to tinker with the internet settings on her laptop.

His eyes glued to the screen, he asked her if she had followed the campus-recommended settings. Anggi, who was quite technology illiterate for one of her age, admitted that she never changed any of her computer's settings. She asked again if he'd had the same problem as her last night; Gio shook his head.

He didn't find anything out of ordinary on her computer, but a system notification was flashing at the bottom-right corner of the screen, saying that the computer was not connected to the internet; the virtual balloon which popped up was advising him to check the modem.

Gio got up and walked to the living room, right next to Anggi's room. The two of them sat down on the cold, wooden floor near the couch, where the device they searched for was located. Three green lights glowed on the black plastic box, but the one labeled "internet" was off. "No wonder," Gio said to Anggi, showing her the cause of her problem.

Perplexed, Anggi told him that the device had been showing as disconnected from the internet continuously since yesterday. She wondered how it had been possible for Gio to surf the internet without any problems. The young man only shrugged in response; he had no idea.

His fingers traced the back of the modem as he looked for the switch to do the generic "off and on again", something he usually did as a first response, when an electronic device suddenly malfunctioned. It wasn't long before all of the green lights on the black device dimmed and went dark, losing their energy. Then, a few seconds later, Gio pressed the power button back on. Like an ancient creature, awakened from its sleep, the modem in front of him opened its five blinking, green eyes, signaling that the interaction portal through space and time had been opened, welcoming all to contact and greet one another.

"There," said Gio, instantly rewarded by a "Thank you" from Anggi.

She then walked back into her room to activate her online chat application, and Gio followed her. On her computer screen, it was apparent that the chat application had quickly reconnected to the virtual world.

"Whoa, it works!" she whooped. "Thank you, Yo."

Gio jokingly said that she owed him lunch, then walked back to his room. From behind his wall, he could make out the voice of Anggi's mother calling out her only daughter's name, followed by Anggi's excited response.

"Anggi! Can you hear me? Is everything alright with you there?"

"Yes, Bu. How are you doing in Indonesia? What time is it there?"

"It's three in the afternoon, darling. Is it nine in the morning there? Has it started to get cold there yet?"

"Yes, Bu, it's nine a.m. here. I have a class at ten but I'm still sleepy," she replied, with a childlike voice which suddenly appeared whenever she spoke to her mother—a funny habit which had persisted for years.

"Well, let's keep this short then, so you won't be late for class. Does your friend Gio also have a class today?"

"Gio doesn't have any more classes, Bu; he's writing his dissertation," replied Anggi.

She heard Gio's bedroom door squeaking, just a meter behind her. She turned her head and saw him standing there, backpack slung over his shoulders and earphone cables dangling from his neck, about to leave.

"Where are you going, Yo?" asked Anggi loudly, from her seat.

Gio pulled out an earphone, so that he could hear her. "Campus." Anggi responded to her friend's reply with a nod.

A sympathetic response came from Anggi's mother, distorted by the internet connection, thousands of kilometers from where Anggi and Gio currently were. *"How are you, Gio? I hear you've been busy with your dissertation."*

"Yes, Tante[26]," Gio replied, from Anggi's doorway.

"Don't believe him, Bu. He's been busy chatting until the wee hours," said Anggi, tattling on him.

Her mother's laugh was heard from the loudspeakers. *"Well, missing your family is okay, isn't it? I, for one, miss this spoilt daughter of mine. Please send my regards to your mother."*

"I chatted with my dad last night, Tante," Gio explained, politely, "but I'll let her know, too."

Anggi locked her gaze on her friend's face, and a few seconds passed, before he said, "Okay, I'd better go now, Tante. Send my regards to Oom[27], at home. Later, 'Gi."

Anggi nodded before turning her attention back to the computer screen, as Gio walked out of the flat and closed the front door loudly behind him, producing an echo which could be heard through the entire building—a sound he was accustomed to hearing, after ten months of living in the private accommodation.

---

[26] "Aunt" in Dutch, used to address older women around one's mother's age.
[27] "Uncle" in Dutch, used to address older men around one's father's age.

"Bu? Hello?" Anggi said, making sure that she was still connected with her mother.

"Yes, darling, I hear you," replied her mother. *"What did Gio say earlier? Did he chat with his mother or his father?"*

Anggi shrugged; "I don't know, Bu."

§

The automatic glass doors opened, and Gio stepped into the large hall of the university's library, on the ground floor. The alma mater's insignia, *"Caledonian University"*, hovered over the heads of its multinational students, who crowded the shop on the ground floor of the library, which had been renovated just the year before.

Gio had just taken an empty seat, beside a glass window sprinkled lightly with autumn rain, when he heard a familiar voice, coming around the rubber-lined earphones hanging over his ears.

"Gio? Are you listening to me?"

"Yes, I'm listening, Pak," the young man replied, dropping his backpack onto the round table in front of him, "but, as I told you before, I've got all the materials for my dissertation, so I can actually work on it in Indonesia."

"Well, in my opinion, it would be better for you to work on your dissertation where you are, Yo. If you need any material, you can get it on campus; it would be a lot more difficult in Indonesia."

"Well, if I need more materials, I can always ask my friends here to help, Pak," Gio insisted.

The voice from inside his ears replied, *"Yo, if you still have any money, instead of spending it on a plane ticket to Indonesia, why not use it to see the rest of 'Sekotlend'. That is, if you're not going to look for a job there."*

"Well..." Gio tried to argue, stifling his laughter at the same time. Hearing the way his father pronounced "Scotland" was one of the many things which made him miss seeing the middle-aged man in the flesh. "I also want to see you."

"You can see me any time after you graduate. Three months is not that long; I can still talk to you by phone."

Gio sighed; he knew that he could never win an argument with his father. His eyes followed the movements of a group of students he saw running into the library, covering their heads from the rain with a book or folder.

"How are you today, Pak? Alright?"

"Alhamdulillah, Yo. I'm—"

Gio's attention was distracted away from his father's voice as a friend tapped his shoulder. Gio turned his head to see Bima, a final semester student from Indonesia, like himself, whom he had met ten months earlier. Behind Bima was a girl Gio had never seen before.

"What are you doing, Yo? Studying?" asked Bima, rubbing his nose—a gesture he always did subconsciously.

"I'm going upstairs in a minute," Gio replied quickly. His gaze wandered to the unfamiliar girl in a black jacket, before again focusing on the man with disheveled hair standing in front of her. "What are *you* doing?"

"I was just showing Widya around the library. Oh, you two haven't met, have you?" said Bima, letting the girl behind him step forward. "This is Widya, a new student in Oil and Gas Engineering. She just came from Indonesia, three days ago."

"Hello." He offered his hand. "Gio."

"Widya," the girl replied, as she took it.

"Please excuse me," Gio said, suddenly remembering the interrupted conversation with his father, "I'm in the middle of a call with my dad."

"Oh, okay," Bima quickly nodded. "The others are meeting for lunch in the canteen. Anggi will be there, too, after her class."

"Okay, I'll be there," promised Gio, raising his hand in a "see you later" gesture, returned in kind by Bima and Widya. After he had watched the two students walking toward the exit door, Gio resumed the conversation with his father.

"Pak? Sorry about that; a friend of mine came over and started talking. So, how are you doing? Are you well?"

"Alhamdulillah, Yo; I'm fine. I have quit smoking for three months now; I no longer have headaches and chest pains."

"Alhamdulillah; I'm so happy to hear that," Gio commented. "Please also watch what you eat, Pak: we don't want your cholesterol level shooting up again."

"Yes, I know." His dad changed the subject. *"But please stop thinking about going home; you should stay where you are until you graduate. Then, after that, you can go home. While you're in Sekotlend, start looking for a job there, if you have time."*

Gio took a deep breath before finally caving in, responding to his dad in a much more resigned tone. "Alright, Pak, I'll go home after graduation. But please take care of your health, okay? We'll talk again tomorrow."

The middle-aged man at the end of the line replied. *"Alright, alright. Take care, 'Le*[28]*."*

Gio promised to do what his father had asked, before finally saying his goodbye and ending the conversation.

§

Bima and Widya were just putting down the plastic tray with their food on it, when they saw Anggi coming toward them, after her class. With her backpack slung over her left shoulder, she made her way amongst the students, milling around the campus cafeteria during lunch hour.

"What are you having?" asked Anggi, seating herself on one of the fiberglass chairs surrounding the table. Bima told her that he had ordered rice and meat, and asked her why she hadn't got anything.

"Later; I'm still stuffed," Anggi replied, before shifting her attention to Widya. "How are you, Wid? How's the weather treating you so far?"

Widya smiled, touched by the young woman's warm welcome. "The wind here is so cold, isn't it? I can't feel my hands. Will I ever get used to this?"

"Never," Anggi and Bima replied in unison, followed by laughter. "I've been here since January and my life still depends on the heater in the flat," Anggi explained. "Ask my flatmate, Gio. Hey, have you met him?"

---

[28] Short for "Tole", used to address younger men and children.

"I have, in the library," Widya nodded, as she chewed her food. "He said he would join us here."

"Oh, okay. He's taking it easy now, since he's soon graduating; he's currently working on his dissertation," Anggi explained.

"When I saw him earlier, he was on a call with his dad," reported Widya.

"His dad?" Anggi questioned.

"Yes," confirmed Widya. This made Anggi raise her eyebrows.

"That's right, Anggi," Bima corroborated her story. "I heard him, too."

Anggi leant closer to Bima, as she recalled earlier, "You know what? He said this morning, too, that he talked to his dad last night."

Bima leant back in his chair and stopped eating his lunch. Meanwhile, Widya, feeling like an outsider in the conversation, asked, "So, what's wrong?"

Anggi and Bima both seemed reluctant to offer an answer. They seemed to be telepathically arguing over which of them should explain. Bima decided to be the one to spell it out.

"Gio's dad passed away, Wid, around three months ago," the young man enlightened his friend.

Widya covered her mouth with her hand. "What? Are you serious?"

"He is, Wid," Anggi vouched for her friend. "Gio's father had been sick for a long time. To make matters worse, his mother forbade Gio from coming home to see him, because his father had always told him not to let anything interrupt his study."

"Gio had insisted on going home at the time, but his mother talked sense into him," added Bima, returning to his nose-rubbing habit. "In the end, he didn't go."

"Oh, my," Widya said, sympathetically. She went quiet for a while, before softly adding, "So… what he said in the library… what did he mean by that?"

Anggi shifted her gaze to the empty table beyond them, and couldn't even begin to think of a reply, while Bima drummed his fingers on the plastic plate in front of him.

"It might have just been a slip of the tongue," Bima speculated; "he probably meant to say he was on a call with his mom. People can easily misspeak, especially when they miss someone. Right?" Both Anggi and Widya seemed to accept Bima's hypothesis.

It was right at that moment that they saw Gio from afar, holding up his hand to them as he walked toward their table. The three of them greeted him in unison as he pulled out one of the chairs and sat down.

"Are you all done with lunch? Sorry, I was caught up on a call with my dad, then I had to borrow some books for my dissertation."

Nobody dared to respond at first. Then, Bima, in the most nonchalant manner he could muster, finally spoke up. "You mean a call with your *mom*, Yo?"

Gio stared at his friend, looking flustered for a second, before he was jolted back to reality. "Oh… yes, *mom*. I meant my mom," he said.

Again, nobody was quick to lead the conversation, as silence engulfed the table of four. Bima quietly finished his lunch, while Anggi and Widya opted to stare at their cellphones, as if expecting some long-awaited message.

§

By midnight, Gio still couldn't rid himself of the nagging belief that he had been talking to his father earlier that day. The logical part of him tried to assure himself that events this morning and the night before had been figments of his own imagination; a manifestation of his longing for his father. His common sense was easily inclined toward this explanation, though the young man was, in truth, disappointed that such an extraordinary moment could be explained away by such simple terminology as "imagination". Another thing making the young man unable to close his eyes, despite the darkness of the room and the cold breeze of the night, was the suspicion that he was starting to lose his grip on reality.

He was still looking at the ceiling when he heard Anggi's voice calling him from outside his room, exactly like this morning. "Yo? Are you still awake?"

Gio took a deep breath before pulling himself up from the mattress, switching on the light and opening his bedroom door. He saw Anggi standing outside, with a look he had now become accustomed to.

"I'm really sorry to bother you again, Yo," she whispered. "It looks like the modem is not working again. I've tried turning it off and on again, like you did this morning, but the internet just won't connect. Just let me know how and I'll try to fix it myself," the girl looked a little uneasy, "or maybe tomorrow, if you're too sleepy to do it now."

"No problem; now is fine," replied Gio, walking out of his bedroom and into the living room where the modem was. For the umpteenth time, he was followed by Anggi's "I'm really sorry, Yo".

After he had once again managed to make all five eyes of the modem blink green, Anggi thanked her friend and they went back to their respective bedrooms. Immediately, from behind his bedroom wall, Gio could hear Anggi chatting with her mother through her online application.

"I miss you, Bu."

"I miss you too, darling. What are you still doing up at this hour? Aren't you tired?" a soft voice replied.

"I am, but I want to chat with you."

On and on, Gio heard their voices replying to one another, permeating through his bedroom wall. Every sentence was welcomed by another from the other side, like a requited embrace.

Spontaneously, he put his earphones in his ears. "Take good care of yourself, okay Pak?" he whispered to his father.

A few seconds went by without him hearing his father's usual chatter, and he knew that his father was alright. And so was he.

THE FOREST PROTECTOR

ALMA

Sometimes, Alma thinks that the human race is not part of this universe, even if, according to the divine revelation from the heavens above, the two came from the same creator. Everything captured by her senses confirms her opinion.

Mankind has been given lands to cultivate, seas to navigate, and skies to admire, yet they betray God's trust by ripping apart the Earth's womb, flooding its oceans with waste and poisoning its skies with smoldering carbon emissions. It seems that this has become the nature of mankind. Every time the aroma of opportunity and desire pervades their soul, humans will bite the hand which feeds them. They want only to taste the joy of breaking the rules.

Perhaps it feels to them like jumping off of a steep ravine, and soon realizing that the ground beneath, which promised instant death, is nothing but a mere painting. Once they know that the things preached to them are nothing but empty threats, the freedom will feel to them like an injection of morphine. Possibilities once taboo will gradually become the new norm. The fear which once sparked at the end of their nerves becomes a craving. Consequences will slowly unravel into myth.

How is it that humans are entrusted to look after the universe when, since the genesis of life, the heavens have refused to take them in? How is it possible for humans to feel like they are the most perfect of creatures, when the very cells which gave life to them can mutate into cancers, which will send them back to their graves? How can the creature glorified as the noblest in the universe be mandated to protect the Earth, when their own bodies and souls are truly the architects of the Apocalypse?

And how can I believe that my limbs will not deceive me? What if they have a mind of their own? What if they make me run away from things? What if they hurt someone else? What if they... kill?

Alma looks at her arms, revealed from underneath the fabric of her now rolled-up shirt sleeves, as if those limbs had been created from parasite incubation, just a few hours ago. The woman can see her 35-year-old knuckles swell, like a pufferfish which has infected itself with its poison. Underneath the tips of her fingernails are red lines, which are sore whenever the wind sweeps over them. On her arms are blackish-red bruises, which might be mistaken for tattoos, from afar. But the tattoos seem like they are alive; they're breathing, pulsing and pumping pains to the neurons in her entire body. Alma scolds her two outstretched arms: *You were the ones that did this, and I get to be the one who feels the pain.*

Out of the blue, like a visit from an unexpected old friend, a voice she recognizes as her own reverberates in her head: *You've become unruly, Alma. You need to be cleansed.*

A memory flashes through her mind, like randomly page-flipping a book on fast-forward. In her mind, she sees shards of glass, and some sort of growling animal, with foamy saliva flowing out of its snout, pain shooting through its body and a violent roar escaping its larynx—it is the roar which disrupts her reverie. Her consciousness brings her back to the toilet cubicle, where she now sits.

You're a disrespectful woman, Alma, she again hears the voice in her head. *You need to be corrected.*

She rolls her eyes to the direction of a razor blade, which she has extracted from its disposable plastic frame. At half an inch long, the shining object lying on top of the ceramic toilet lid she sits on seems to be luring her into picking it up and using it. *"Expel the poison from your body, Alma. Cleanse yourself,"* she hears herself murmur. Or was it the razor blade?

No! Alma tries to fight back.

She tries to remember the small face which stared at her, innocently, when he saw the drying scabs on the skin of her arms. "What happened to your arms?" the face had asked her.

Looking into his eyes, she knew that the child could not grasp the meaning behind what he saw, but he looked worried. After all, even a child knows that wounds and cuts are not a nice thing to happen to a person.

"But this will cleanse your sins, Alma," the wicked voice airs again. *"And, God loves those who wash their sins away. He loves His humble people."*

The motionless, steel blade beside her now seems to slash toward her corneas. She closes her eyes. In the darkness, she can see the face of her child, asking her again, "Did Ayah[29] do this to you, Bunda[30]?"

"No." Alma remembers she gave him the truthful answer. "Not Ayah." She remembers that she had replied as casually as she could, "Belang scratched me."

"I'll scold Belang for this," her son responded. His cat-chat, which usually made her laugh, now made her want to curl up and cry at the edge of the Earth.

"You see? The deceitful larvae have long dwelled inside your veins. Your son will never know. Nobody will know. Nobody has known this whole time, anyway, have they?"

Alma stares again at the inviting razor blade.

Just this one time, she makes a pact with herself, although she's not sure if she will be able to see it through, another few hours from now. *This will be the last time, then I won't have to do it again. There will be no more cleansing of sins.*

Besides, what more can I cleanse, when the most shameful and disgraceful sin has poured out of me, dissolved and been sucked into the drain?

She doesn't remember when she picked up the blade from atop the toilet lid, but she is now holding the rectangular object, just a few centimeters from her eyes. She can see the clear, sharp edge of the blade, as if it has just been honed by a blacksmith. Just looking at it makes the scars on her arms raw again—wet and glittery, just like the first time they were carved.

---

[29] Dad.

[30] Mom.

Just one slash; just until the damned fluid trickles out. New blood cells will be born, washing my organs with God's grace.

Alma is just about to pierce the soft skin of her arm with the tip of the blade when a voice calls from outside the closed door. "Bunda?"

Jolted from her trance, Alma gasps. She immediately hides the blade behind her, though she knows nobody can see. "Yes, honey?" she replies, unrolling her shirt sleeve to hide her scars from the world's judgmental eyes.

"Are you going to be long?" Alma hears her son asking from behind the door

"I'm done. Hang on a second, okay, honey?" Alma replies.

The mother stands up from the toilet bowl, pulls the tank lever sticking out of its side, and gives the impression that she was emptying her bladder for the past half an hour, rather than deliberating whether she should carve her arms with a razor blade, as usual. The sound of water gushing out of the tank and filling the bowl is thunderous to her ears, and flushes away the urge for her sin-cleansing ritual. Right away, she slides the metal bolt from its slot and opens the door.

RAFA

When his mother opens the toilet cubicle door, in response to his knocking, Rafa sees the pretty face that he has always admired. But the expression now on that pretty face shows him that something is off—as if his mother has just woken from a long slumber, and a piece of her soul has been left in another realm. "Rafa, what are you doing here?" his mother asks.

Rafa sees droplets of water—or is it perspiration?—on his mother's chest and armpits, seeping through the white, long-sleeved shirt she is wearing. The small buttons at the ends of her sleeves are free from their holes, flapping around in the air, like a bird taken from its nest, every time Alma moves her arms.

"I told you to wait outside," she tells him. "This is the ladies' room."

"You took so long, I thought you'd left already," the boy replies.

Ushering him out of the toilet, his mother responds, "That's impossible, isn't it? This is the only way in or out. Besides, there's no way I would leave without telling you."

Outside, Alma and Rafa walk over to their black, tubular bag, lying on the railway-station's floor. The boy hears his mother's hysterical shriek as she sees the bag unattended. She asks him what if someone had taken it. "All of our clothes and stuff are in there," she says.

"Not everything," he protests, "we didn't bring along my toys and comic books." Rafa sees his mother not bothering to respond to his protest, although he is sure she must have heard it. A sliver of sadness stings his heart, as the little man recalls his troops of robots and superheroes from unknown galaxies—all were left on the shelves in his bedroom. Those magical knights now seem thousands of lightyears away from the railway station he is now in. It feels to him like leaving behind loyal best friends, who have been there for him every day and night—especially at night—when the ruckus outside his room made him too scared to peek.

But, what makes him scowl the most as he now looks at his mother's face, is the fact that she made him leave his beloved comic books on the desk and underneath his mattress. He imagines his favorite characters—Dewandara, the zombie-annihilating gravekeeper; Nalyawira, the librarian who exterminates giant bugs in the city sewers; and, Mahardika, the veteran explorer, who eradicates the forest-destroying phantoms—continuing their adventures without him. He feels his mother has taken away all the things in his life which made him happy.

Ah, he suddenly remembers, *Ayah can bring me my toys and comic books when he comes later.* The little man asks his mother when his father will catch up with them in the city.

He watches the woman kneel before him, before she replies, "Your glasses are so dirty."

He doesn't get to see her expression following her response to his question, because his mother has lifted the temples of his gray glasses from his ears and taken them off of his head. His eye muscles weaken at once, as any solid object placed before him turns into a trace of a ghost, including his mother's face.

"How is it possible that an eight-year-old is wearing minus-eight glasses already?" he hears Alma grumbling, as she cleans the lenses. "It's because you read those comics all the time. No more reading comic books when we get to Grandma's house, okay?"

"Well, all my comic books are at home," Rafa retorts. The only reaction he receives from his mother is her hands putting the glasses back on him, sitting the pads on the top of his nose and the arms over his ears.

Afterward, half-running, the little man follows his mother's quick steps. They pass the long benches where passengers wait for their train's arrival to be announced, heading toward the gate manned by a uniformed staff member who will check their tickets. It appears that the city-bound train has arrived at platform 5, and passengers are heading in that direction, now welcomed to board the carriages.

While the staff check their tickets, Rafa sees his mother turning her head around, looking at the hundreds of other queuing passengers, as if for someone in particular. Then, after the staff in the brightly colored uniform before them tells them to board, Rafa feels his mother's hand pushing against his back, as if prompting him to walk faster. He concludes that his mother was not looking for someone in the crowd; rather, she was *avoiding* someone.

§

Series of hills, valleys and fields, seen from the windows, seem like an endless painting, rolling backward, as the train which takes Alma and Rafa to the country's capital city cuts through the air. Rafa leans his head against the leather-covered seat, whilst looking at the panorama displayed on the window-screen.

Through the pair of rubber-padded earphones plugged into his ears, he listens to a song from his music player. The beat of the tune, which he has listened to hundreds of times—the theme song for a superhero named *Mahardika*—and the rumble of the train's engine, which sounds as if it moves by simply crushing the rocks underneath, create a monotonous rhythm, which makes his mind wander, looking for something else to keep itself busy.

He tries to remember what happened earlier this morning. He thinks that his morning began just like any other ordinary Sunday. He had been awake since six o'clock, but had kept his eyes closed, just to feel the soothing mattress which cradled him, and his remaining sleepiness, which was starting to fade away.

Vaguely, he had heard noises from downstairs, where the dining room, kitchen and living room were. At first, it was only dishes clanging and clinking together—Rafa concluded that his mother was preparing breakfast in the kitchen. But then his ears had caught another sound: his father talking and his mother responding. He couldn't make out what they were talking about. From where he was, his parents' voices sounded like they were coming out of muffled mouths—distant and faint. But the little man could recognize the bitter tone surrounding every word coming out of his father's mouth, as if each had an energy of its own, which could change the molecules in the air, making the very atmosphere around him feel suffocating. The same smothering climate seemed also to possess his mother; he heard the same bitterness in his mother's voice, as she retorted in high decibels.

"I'm not stupid; I know where you've been going to."

"What's that supposed to mean?" Rafa heard his father ask.

Then, Alma made a sound he had never heard before, a kind of laugh which sounded like a cry. At once, he felt as if his insides had turned to stone.

"Don't play dumb. You didn't stay there until the very end."

Like a crescendo, he heard his father's voice growing higher. He reiterated what he had been explaining to her since yesterday: he would be in the restaurant all night, right up until the end of the event because last night was his boss's farewell party.

"And, watch your mouth!" his father rebuked.

Impulsively, he tucked himself deeper into his blanket, wishing that the shadows surrounding him could suck him out of the house and fling him into a world made entirely of ink and pixels, where all shouting, punching and pain were forever locked inside boxy panels on paper.

"*You* watch what *you're* doing!" he heard his mother snap in a hoarse voice. "What kind of example are you setting for Rafa?"

Please, Bunda, stop talking. Please, anybody, don't say anything. Please, everyone, stop... Rafa found himself repeating the same words over and over in his head, like a mantra, because he knew exactly what his father was capable of when the man lost his temper. But the mantra didn't appear potent enough.

"What kind of example are *you* trying to give Rafa? How to be a lunatic?" it wasn't long until his father retorted.

Please, Bunda, don't answer him... please don't answer...

"I'm showing him an example of how *not* to be a cowardly man."

At once, he knew that his mother had just thrown a flaming matchstick into an oil puddle. He heard something hitting a surface then breaking, followed by a curse which he didn't understand, but sounded terrifying when roared wildly by his father.

The little man's body was suddenly stricken by something strange: his whole body shook uncontrollably, as if the blanket which wrapped him was made of snow; his breathing became sharp whispers and his fingers shrunk, as if looking for warmth inside his skin.

Underneath the blanket, his eyes looked for anything which could stop his body from shaking.

Then, he remembered something. Like a tentacle, he reached his hand out from under the blanket, to feel along the surface of the desk next to his bed. When he was sure that his hand had found what he was looking for, he pulled it back under the blanket. A rectangular, light-blue music-playing device sat in the palm of his hand; the cable, which forked into a pair of rubber-lined earbuds, coiled like a tapeworm in his grip. Plugging his ears with the earphones, he pressed a button on his music player. All at once, the ruckus in the house was shooed away, by the music booming against his ear-drums.

"Born out of the flame of the forest,
Stinging like a tarantula,
His eyes as sharp as the King of the Jungle,
Here comes Mahardika, the Forest Protector...
Ooh... Mahardika, the Forest Protector..."

Rafa closed his eyes, trying to bury himself in scenes of Mahardika, fighting all kinds of demons and goblins in the forest, to the beats and rhythms of the theme song. Every punch landed by the forest protector, onto the pus-smeared face of the monster, was always in sync with the wailing sound of the guitar. Every kick from his hard-as-iron leg, which landed on the bodies of the forest-destroying phantoms, was accompanied by the sounds of adrenaline-inducing percussion. Watching Mahardika beating up and finishing off the phantom intruders weakened his muscles entirely; terror and tremors no longer gripped him. He felt his world was now safe from any threats and everything was alright.

But then, without warning, a force grabbed the blanket covering the head of the little man and was yanked away, to reveal his whole body, curled up on top of the mattress like a baby. He opened his eyes, startled by the sudden change.

In his view, he saw a figure whom at first he didn't recognize, because the expression embedded in her face was terrifying.

"Bunda?" he finally murmured, hesitantly.

His mother's face looked like she had just seen something which her mind couldn't fathom; she looked dumbfounded. Her hair, disheveled, almost hid her entire face. Her arms looked like they had been dipped in red ink, but he didn't remember to ask where the red had come from. And, although hidden underneath the vines of her hair, he could see that his mother's pupils had shrunk to the size of a watermelon seed, making the woman look like one of the zombies he often saw on the pages of his comic books.

"Pack your stuff, Rafa. We're going to Oma[31]'s," his mother commanded.

"Now," Alma added before he could ask the questions which manifested in his head.

The stern note in his mother's voice made him immediately jump off of his bed to grab his backpack, and he started to pack.

He remembered Alma asking him to pack only essential things, like clothes and personal effects; "No toys," his mother reminded him, before she left his bedroom.

---

[31] "Grandma" in Dutch.

Not long after, she was back in his room with a clean face, her hair tied into a ponytail, wearing a white, long-sleeved shirt and holding a black gym bag, which he was sure had been filled with his mother's stuff. Alma put some of his remaining clothes into her gym bag, then, when she was sure that they had packed everything they would need, she told Rafa to follow her downstairs.

When their two pairs of feet reached the third step of the stairs, his mother suddenly seemed to remember something. Turning to him, she reached out her hand.

"Rafa," she said, "take off your glasses."

ALMA

She never understands why, in her mind, something as amazing as watching the sun rise and set on the horizon, or observing coral reefs at the bottom of the sea, always manages to slow the Earth's rotation, making her feel as though she has more time to take in all of the wonders before her. On the contrary, time seems to speed up when something unpleasant is happening, as if the Earth wants to run away from the danger and hide in a safe place, too.

What happened this morning, a mere few hours ago, now seems like pieces of an incomplete picture in her mind. But the throbbing black-and-blue marks on her cheeks, shoulders and tailbone are sending sufficient pain signals to her central nervous system to help her recall very clearly what happened.

She remembers her husband throwing her body to the floor with one jerk of his hand. When she lost her balance, it was as if the world around her had swollen, intimidating her; swallowing her up. She screamed in agony when her lower back hit the floor; pain exploded inside her like fireworks, paralyzing her for a moment.

Amidst her pain, she could see the man approaching her. He seemed larger than usual, as if anger had transformed the physiology of his body into a creature from Hell, thirsty for blood. Her husband walked over to her with firm steps, doubling as the Grim Reaper—like a tiger coming for its prey. He knelt down, watching her lying helpless on the floor, frozen in fear.

She couldn't breathe when her husband's two hands grabbed the skin underneath her armpits, lifting her up to a standing position. Then, with one jerk, he slammed her back against the towering refrigerator behind her. His hands were now clamping her neck, blocking the oxygen craved by all the cells in her body.

"Watch your mouth, bitch," he growled, disgusting veins snaking up his temples. His stare was so pitiless that she believed she might die, right there and then, in his hands.

"I've tried to be patient, but you're out of line this time. Your mouth needs to learn some manners," she heard her husband saying in a hoarse voice.

Her brain couldn't make sense of a single thing the man was saying. She felt like she was in an upside-down world; doubts were swirling in her mind, slowly crushing her stance. *Am* I *the crazy one? Am* I *the one to blame for speaking to him that way? If I had not spoken to him like that, he wouldn't be doing this to me. I shouldn't have gone looking for trouble.*

Then, a face of innocence once again illuminated her mind. Rafa was so pure, free from any intent or desire, other than to play with his superhero figurines and read his comic books. She didn't want her beloved son to lose his innocence which had, until now, protected him from the sharp fangs of the world. She didn't want him paralyzed by fear and anxiety—to surrender to the threat of a monster, like she had.

Thinking about all the evil things which threaten her son's life made her cry, but she hated it when she realized she was showing vulnerability to her husband. Still, she couldn't contain her emotions. The harder she tried to stop her tears, the louder she sobbed.

Convinced that his threat had poisoned her soul, the man loosened his grip on his wife's neck. Whilst at it, he also imparted a lecture, for good measure. "If you want other people to respect you, learn to respect others. Understand? Everything has its consequences. If you treat people like shit, don't be surprised when you're treated the same."

She felt her brain boiling, and her body spontaneously writhed and thrashed around, trying to protect her dying soul. Unabashed, she roared, not caring who might hear. Meanwhile, her hands were flailing behind her, toward the kitchen utensils, scattered at the bottom of the sink—the clattering of iron, porcelain and aluminum dishes crashing on top of one another could not drown out her screaming. Finally, her hand managed to grab onto something made of wood. The sound of metallic sliding filled the air as Alma yanked the object out of the stack of utensils. With a mighty swing of her hand, she lashed out at her husband.

Her clenched hand, tight around the wooden handle, impacted with her husband's left shoulder—along with the blade of the knife protruding from it. The blade's sharp tip easily pierced through the fabric of his shirt and the skin underneath. His torn artery squirted blood, which quickly drenched the body of the man standing before her like a blot of ink.

Though the red liquid also soaked her knife-holding hand, whilst witnessing all of this, she didn't flinch at all; her eyes were accustomed to the color of blood. Her skin was no longer squeamish at the sight of a red flood; her nose was familiar with the sweet aroma now tickling her olfactory nerves.

The only thing which captured her attention now was the expression creeping over the face of the man in front of her. For the first time, she caught a new color in her husband's face. At first, the man looked stunned, as if his mind hadn't been able to digest what was happening. As a few minutes passed, his eyeballs seemed to enlarge. Consciousness, pain and fear coiled in his nerves, commanding his right hand to comfort the source of his pain.

Alma immediately pulled the knife out of her husband's shoulder, making way for the red, life-carrying liquid to pour out more easily.

The agonized wail now coming out of the man in front of her broke the silence. This time, his voice sounded vulnerable and cornered—no longer feral. Along with it, she saw her husband staggering backward, losing his balance. His left arm, which was now drenched in blood, reached out limply to her face, as if trying to tear it off.

She stepped back, dropped the knife, and spontaneously grabbed for a bigger object. She could hear the loud, heartbreaking clang when the cast-iron pan she swung hit her husband's skull, sending him to the floor, motionless.

She felt as if all of the air had been sucked out of her lungs. Suddenly, she no longer had the ability to stand, and she threw herself backward against the closed refrigerator doors, letting gravity pull her body down to the floor. Once she hit the floor, it felt like every liter of oxygen in the air was being shoved down her throat by invisible hands. The heart in her ribcage sounded like a beating drum in her ears, as if the blood in her body was rebelling in its very atria and ventricles, trying to force its way out.

As if pulled by a magnet, her eyes remained locked on the body, now lying still on the floor, like a newly slaughtered animal. The two arms connected to the body were spread wide, as if waiting for the Grim Reaper's embrace. His goggle eyes made him look like somebody who was still having a nightmare, whilst wide awake. The pupils, no longer responding to light, stared in her direction, making Alma feel naked.

Shut your eyes, you bastard! she barked, internally. But her husband's eyes kept looking at her, as if they could only be forever hers when he had become a corpse. She turned away, but could still feel those eyes following her every move, as if she were the most wonderful wife on Earth. Or the most despicable...

She didn't want to let her husband continue to annoy her, even in his death. Trembling, she grabbed a carelessly folded towel from the sink and threw it toward the expressionless face on the floor. The shabby fabric drifted in the air for a long second, before landing right on top of her husband's face. Right then and there, she felt protected from the corpse's judgment; her breathing flowed easier and her heartbeat slowed, even though she was sure she had seen her husband's eyes move, right at the moment before the towel covered his face.

§

The vibration of the train's wheels rolling along the steel railway sends her soul back into her body, sitting in the carriage. The other passengers around her also seem carried away by the gentle tremor tickling the train's pace. Some are asleep, with their heads propped up against the window, letting the rhythmic sway of the train lull them, though many pairs of eyes seem to be looking at smartphone screens, with varied levels of intensity. Some seem to be deep in concentration, trying to absorb information. But many only stare passively at the device, as if the instruments in their hands are merely masks for their daydreaming or other internal time-killing activity. Alma wonders if, amongst the hundreds of passengers inside these carriages, there are any filthy people like her: a murderer.

She feels an odd sensation as the label crosses her mind. She had never thought the horrible moniker would ever be applied to her. She repeats the word in her mind. *Murderer*. She shudders, ashamed and disgusted with every cell molding her physique.

She looks over at Rafa, who sits to her right, staring at the view flashing by outside the window. Both of his ears are plugged with his rubber-lined, music-playing earbuds, placing the boy in his own fantasy land, hidden from the restlessness of the adults around him.

Alma suddenly can't believe that she ever thought she could now raise Rafa alone, especially considering what she had done this morning. She doesn't deserve to be a mother. The same hands which bathe her son every day have now become instruments of death; the same fingers which stroke her son's forehead every night, before sleep, have become nightmare-bearing claws; her tongue, which always tells her beloved boy to do the right thing, and to always be courageous, has become a lie-spreading tool.

Who can guarantee that you won't kill again, next time you can't control your rage? Who can guarantee that your son won't end up as the next lifeless body, staring blankly at you from the bloodstained floor?

Like an accumulation of waste the Earth can't degrade, her troubles now pile up to the surface of her face, contaminating it with furrows and sweat, until she hears her son's voice again…

RAFA

"What's wrong, Bunda?"

Again, he finds the same expression he has seen on his mother's face all day since this morning: blank and not paying attention, as if the substances which gave her life suddenly won't stick to her skin. He sees her reacting emotionally to his question before she responds. "Nothing."

"Are you sick?" he asks again.

His mother shakes her head. "No," she replies. But her eyes seem to be encased in a layer of crystal membrane, which she immediately rubs dry with her fingers; the boy knows at once that his mother is holding back tears.

"Are you hungry?" she asks, with a voice which suddenly sounds calm. He shakes his head. His mother asks one more time if he wants to eat in the dining car, and once again he shakes his head.

"I'm not hungry," the boy says.

He hears his mother take a deep breath and say, "Okay," but the little man assumes she is mumbling to herself.

Then, as if silence is a source of horror to his mother, he hears her voice again, after a while. "What are you listening to?"

Unable to hide his longing and admiration of the superhero, Rafa spells out the complete title of the theme song playing in his ears. "'Mahardika, the Forest Protector'."

The boy's response seems to ignite a glimmer of memory in Alma's head. The woman suddenly reaches for the gym bag underneath the seat and sinks her hand into it, through the unzipped part. He can see long lines of scarring on his mother's arm. Some scars are dark brown and no longer seem terrifying, but others are still the same color as blood and seem to sizzle when they come into contact with anything. He abruptly shifts his gaze up to his mother's face.

"Speaking of Mahardika..." Alma pulls something from the bag, letting it sit in her hand to complete her sentence.

The boy immediately recognizes the figure in the green vest, whose body is forever locked in a heroic stance—thanks to the factory setting—ready to deploy his deadly moves on the forest-disrupting ghouls. Even in his plastic, 3-inch posture, Mahardika looks gallant in Rafa's eyes. The little man shrieks joyfully and grabs his favorite toy from his mother's hand. Alma can't hide her surprise when her son spreads his arms wide and hugs her. "Thank you, Bunda," he says, followed by a ripple of laughter which chases the gray clouds away from her heart.

He looks at Mahardika, now right in front of him, still in awe, as if the figurine in his hand really has a potent power, and that all of his confusion, worries and fears are forgotten, even if only for a while. The little man feels like he has just been given the key to the universe, where he can feel as important, powerful and brave as his superhero. Adrenaline bangs against his heart as he listens to the *Mahardika* theme song, which now feels as if it is being sung just for him.

"His roar makes the phantoms tremble.
He's a mighty warrior, powerful beyond compare.
His signature move, fatal and deadly.
Call his name: Mahardika, the Forest Protector.
Ooh... Mahardika, the Forest Protector."

ALMA

Seeing her son engrossed in his fantasy world, leaving all the ugliness of the real world behind, makes her breathe easier.

Slowly, she explores a new idea. The human race is not only an integral part of the universe, but essentially the source of food for the Earth, which, with its boiling magma, rolling rainstorms and plates which constantly crack open, chew and digest the human corpses, until they turn to dust. It is from this dust that new human beings will be born, to carry out the mandate the Earth has given them: to sacrifice other human beings every time it feels hungry.

Monsters.

The Earth is full of monsters. And she swears to protect Rafa from its ancient, outstretched claws.

MY HEIRLOOM, YOU'LL BE

The mother's eyes widened when she saw her son fornicating with a dishonourable woman. Fajar's chest, covered in sweat, moved in unison with the swing of his pelvis. His lust was boiling, triggered by the sighs of Ambar's breath. The woman, lying on her back on the passenger seat, stretched her neck, whispering Fajar's name every now and then as if every jolt of the man's body brought her infinite pleasure. Ambar really understood how to intoxicate her lover. It didn't matter if Ambar didn't actually feel the same joy. Fajar wasn't adept at making love, but Ambar thought he had the right to taste what it felt like to be a stud. After all, Fajar had been good to her.

"This belongs to my mother," Fajar said as he wrapped a gold chain necklace around Ambar's neck just before they shuffled into the passenger seat. Having never had luxurious jewellery before, Ambar's eyes were stunned by the gleam emanating from every tiny link that formed the piece. However, what caught her attention was the bulging eye—or at least that was her first impression—which was hanging from the end of the necklace chain. White diamond shards clustered around the emerald piece, holding it hostage in the middle, forcing the eye to see it all.

"Are you sure your mother would want you to give this to me?"

"Of course," Fajar assured her. There was no doubt on his face, "in fact, she specifically asked me to give it to you."

Ambar raised her eyebrow in disbelief. Considering their relationship wasn't exactly the type that a Javanese traditionalist mother would approve of, this unexpected gift came as a pleasant surprise to Ambar.

I guess I am welcome to the family after all, Ambar thought. But then again, she supposed Fajar's mother just had no choice in the matter.

Ambar's attention shifted back to the present, where Fajar, now moving faster above her, grunted in pleasure as he climaxed. Out of breath, Fajar collapsed on Ambar's shoulder, feeling worthy of an embrace even after only satisfying himself.

Ambar stroked Fajar's hair as if she was lulling a child to sleep, while her mind wandered, contemplating everything that had brought her here.

"Ambar, are there no single men in your office?" Ambar remembered her mother had asked a few weeks ago during dinner.

Careful not to rise to her mother's taunt, Ambar chose to take a piece of tofu that was laid out on the table. But as expected, her mother never waited for an answer.

"Not one man has approached you at work? Or maybe you scare them away?"

Ambar didn't have enough patience that day. "Mom, would they hire me as their secretary if they thought I would scare people away? And my priority there is not to find a husband."

"Just remember, you'll only get older," the mother replied, always scapegoating time as the enemy, "you'll be in your thirties this year. If you don't start looking for a husband now, when will you get one?"

"I just got a *job*, Mom," Ambar stressed every word as if talking to a child, "can I focus on that first?"

But her mother didn't relent, "I'm not telling you to quit your job. I'm just saying that, while working, you can also search for a husband. Your fortune will only grow after you get married. Didn't you read the *hadith*[32] book I gave you?"

Ambar's face heated up. *If getting married can make you rich, why were we always poor when Dad was still alive?* Ambar was about to respond, but chose to clear the plates from the table and withdraw from the battlefield. In her mind, she wished to get enough money fast to afford her own place, so she would no longer be trapped with her mother, although this thought made her feel like an ungrateful daughter. It wouldn't matter anyway. Ambar knew that her salary as a secretary in a small law firm wouldn't be able to buy the freedom that she longed for.

However, that night, as she lay on her bed, considering her options, Ambar thought that maybe it could be helpful for her to have a boyfriend. She wouldn't give a rat's ass if she fancied the guy. At least his presence could, for a time, stop her mother's nagging comments every night.

---

[32] A record of the Islamic prophet Muhammad's words, actions, and approval.

Hence, in her first few weeks at work, Ambar began to look for a potential mate. It was clear to her that Fajar stood out from the rest, and it wasn't because of his position. Well, not *entirely* anyway. Because even though Fajar was the owner and partner of the law office she worked in, he was different from most other young entrepreneurs in similar positions, in that he wasn't an entitled jerk. If anything, Ambar saw that Fajar was too naïve to use his power. He could only make decisions after getting validation from others, including his subordinates. Ambar could often hear Fajar's questions to the associate lawyers in his office: *Could you check the law, have we quoted them right? What is the name of the law again? So, we've quoted the correct one, right? Does this report look good enough to you?*

It was clear to Ambar that Fajar was her "in". While physically, Fajar was definitely not her type, Ambar found his habit of always asking for others' opinions refreshing. Ambar imagined it must be nice to be with someone who cared about what she had to say. She wanted to know more about him, but in the two weeks she had been working there, Ambar had only been trusted with filing and scanning documents. The rest, the man did himself. Accustomed to fighting to get what she wanted, Ambar knew that she had to be proactive.

One afternoon at work, when all the other secretaries had gone home, Ambar knocked on Fajar's office door and stepped inside. From behind the pile of documents on the desk, he looked up.

"Excuse me, Mas Fajar. Is there anything I can help you with?" Ambar's voice sounded sweet, surprising even herself. "Is it okay if I call you 'Mas'? You're still quite young, so I thought..."

Fajar didn't answer right away; he just stared at her. Ambar panicked. Was I too forward? Perhaps he would like me more if I just acted pretty and cute like all the other secretaries here?

For a moment, Ambar suspected that maybe there was something wrong with the way she dressed. But that day, she was wearing a blazer, white shirt, and black pleated skirt. An ensemble that was very common in a workplace, if not boring.

Ambar was about to apologize and shuffle out of the room before Fajar asked, "It's already late; you don't want to go home instead?"

"I don't have anything to do at home anyways," Ambar said.

Fajar smiled awkwardly. His previous secretary had never been this straightforward. He motioned for Ambar to sit down, with Fajar's desk stretched between them like a barricade. He handed a document to Ambar and commented that the format therein wasn't up to the firm's standard. Fajar had asked a junior lawyer to fix it, but the young man had to go home early due to a family emergency.

"I have to send this out to our client tonight." Fajar tried to sound calm, though Ambar could see the nervous twitch on his face. Fajar asked Ambar to tidy up the formatting on the executive summary, while Fajar would check on the regulatory references.

"If I may, can I just bring my laptop here?" Ambar asked, which prompted a doubtful look from her superior. Ambar quickly gave her justification, "So that if I have any questions, I can just discuss them with you here instead of having to go back and forth into the room."

Fajar thought her reasoning was quite sensible. In the hours that followed, Ambar worked across the table from Fajar in his office, typing away on the laptop in front of her. Every now and then, Ambar would read a series of paragraphs from the file to him, making sure her revisions were in accordance with his wishes. From the spelling of terminologies that were foreign to her (*juncto, lex specialis,* and *pacta sunt servanda,* to name a few), cross-references to things that piqued her curiosity ("Why is the law changed so many times? How can they expect us to keep up?" "Why can't the regulations use a simpler language?" "So lawyers are basically just copying off of the law with a little bit of paraphrasing?"). At first, Fajar just answered dismissively, as if he thought that Ambar would eventually lose interest. However, as the secretary's questions became more and more probing, Fajar's answers became more detailed. There was no longer any hesitation in his voice. Ambar saw, to her delight, that Fajar had started to enjoy conversing with her. She suspected that his confidence emerged after he was sure that Ambar wouldn't doubt his words. She began to think that, like herself, perhaps Fajar just wanted somebody to act as a sounding board.

Ambar found other similarities with Fajar when they had dinner together at a cafe after working until late at night for the umpteenth time.

"Even after I opened my own law office, my mother still complained, 'Why don't you try working for a bona fide company first to build your resume?', 'My friends' kids work in oil and gas companies offshore, and they got good benefits and everything,'" Fajar tried to sound humorous. Still, Ambar knew, even in the dim light of the cafe, that these comments had been bothering him for a long time.

"My mother is the same way, Mas," Ambar said. "I thought she would be happy when she found out I got a job. But her complaints just shift to 'When are you getting married?' and so on."

Both of them laughed, relieved to know that they belonged to the same clan: grown humans who only functioned as extensions of their parents.

Fajar said that his mother also often tried to set him up with her friends' daughters. "She asked me to have dinner with her friend's daughter tomorrow. Her father is a director of a state-owned company," Fajar said.

Not knowing what to say, Ambar just nodded at first. However, when she caught the tired look on Fajar's face, Ambar asked, "If you don't feel like it, why don't you just refuse to go?"

Fajar stared at Ambar as if she had just said something ridiculous. A defeated smile spread across his face. "Even if we refuse, do you think our mothers would stay silent?"

Ambar recalled her mother's complaints whenever they argued about her future: "I know this is none of my business. But is it wrong for a mother to want the best for her daughter?" "Have I ever asked anything from you? Why can't you just listen to what I say for once?", "Remember the *hadith*, Ambar. Children must make their parents happy."

Ambar returned Fajar's smile, raised her glass, and toasted. "May your matchmaking dinner go splendidly tomorrow."

Ambar thought her humour was too grim for most people, but Fajar laughed out loud at her direct remarks. She realized that she liked seeing him laugh.

But it wouldn't change a thing anyway, since Ambar realized that her chances of winning her lottery were slim. She knew that there was no way a devout prince could defy the mandate of his queen mother.

Which was why Ambar was surprised when she saw Fajar the next day, still in his office at 8 p.m. From her cubicle, Ambar could see him in his room, which was entirely framed by glass partitions. He was sitting in the chair; his eyes were glued to the monitor. But Ambar knew the man wasn't paying attention to anything. His mind was lost in the ether, which Ambar had often caught him doing whenever he thought nobody was watching. Triggered by curiosity, Ambar stepped into Fajar's office, but not before taking a document from her desk to make her visit look more official.

Fajar's gaze shifted to Ambar as she entered. Ambar could see his face beamed at the sight of her—which she thought was cute.

"Don't you have a dinner date tonight?" Ambar immediately retorted.

Hearing Ambar's question, Fajar's brow furrowed. "I have an online meeting tonight with a Panamanian company."

For a moment, a sense of panic hit Ambar. *How could I forget that he has a work meeting tonight?* Ambar had always prided herself on being good at keeping track of things. This carelessness made Ambar curse at herself in her head, in a voice identical to her mother's. But then she remembered something.

"I don't recall us having a client from Panama, Mas."

Fajar's smile slowly grew. "If you ask my mother and my date now, they think we have."

Ambar couldn't hold back her laughter. It was endearing to her to see the changes in Fajar's demeanour over the last few weeks. Like herself, the man was twisting and turning, trying to free himself from his shackles. However, Ambar knew that any struggle was futile. They were lifetime debtors to their mothers, and pursuing desires other than their matriarch's wishes would constitute a default.

Ambar and Fajar had dinner together again that night, and the night after that. And the night after that. Their conversations always lasted until the café was closed, and Fajar always drove her home afterward. She knew that they had become the subject of gossip throughout the office, from secretaries to employees to the partners' level. Everybody must have noticed that Ambar was the only secretary who was still in her cubicle after five o'clock in the afternoon and that she would only leave the office when Fajar finished working.

"Maybe I should just wait for you on the ground floor," Ambar suggested one afternoon.

Fajar refused and asked her not to care about what other people said. "I have learned not to bother anymore, Ambar. And you should too. It's liberating."

Ambar reminded him that as the owner and the management in the office, he might remain safe from any consequences, at least for now, but not for a secretary who only had been working there for a month. And she was not planning to lose her job.

"I'm the founding partner in this office, Ambar. If anyone has to worry about their position in this office, it's them."

Ambar raised her eyebrows, surprised. If someone had said to her that the timid man she knew a month ago was the same person as the man who now sat in Fajar's office, Ambar would never have believed them. However, she felt a sense of pride, like a mother's, seeing the burgeoning man she had created.

Fajar drove Ambar home again that night, stopping just outside the alley where her house was. She didn't want her mother to know that her boss drove her home every night. Ambar knew that even though her mother always wanted her to find a mate, making sure her only daughter avoided adultery and *especially* being the subject of nasty gossiping by the neighbours was paramount. Regarding why she often came home late, Ambar always reasoned to her mother that working overtime was something common in a law office, even for the secretaries. Her mother never once questioned Ambar's excuses, at least for now.

"I told my mother about us," Fajar said. His gaze fell on their intertwined hands. "I hope that's okay."

Ambar was disappointed that Fajar did this without asking her first. The old Fajar, Ambar was sure, would have asked for her opinion first before telling anyone else about their relationship.

Now that the queen mother had been made aware that her young prince had secretly been getting intimate with a peasant woman, Ambar could only guess which one of them would be called a whore. Bitterness permeated her mind, so thick that she could taste it on her tongue.

"What did you say to her?" Ambar asked, preparing for the worst.

"I showed her your picture. She said that you're beautiful and wanted to meet you," Fajar said.

Bullshit.

"What else did you not tell me?"

Fajar seemed stunned by Ambar's reaction. "What do you mean?"

At that moment, Ambar found his naïveté exasperating. "Even if your mother wants to see me, it's definitely not because she likes me. She probably wants to prove how unworthy I am."

Despite her protest, Ambar knew that meeting the queen mother was something she couldn't avoid, especially if she wanted their relationship to attain legitimacy. As of now, she knew that she was already floating on her space shuttle, halfway to escaping her prison. She just hoped that she would not be denied permission to land.

Fajar whispered, as if able to read her mind, "Ambar, you don't have to worry. Even if my mother doesn't like you, she won't be able to do much."

Ambar looked at Fajar, waiting for him to make his point.

"My mother is very sick."

Fajar's voice broke as if shards of glass were puncturing his throat. He told Ambar that his mother had stage four colon cancer. Her condition had deteriorated rapidly since she was first diagnosed with the disease two months ago. Even though she had undergone resection surgery, doctors still found cancer cells left in her body, so she had to continue with a series of chemotherapy.

Fajar said that his mother didn't respond well to the drugs. On the doctor's advice, Fajar decided that his mother be treated palliatively at home with the help of a nurse. Ambar knew exactly what this meant: only divine intervention could save the queen from death.

Unfortunately, Ambar knew from her own experience with her late father that the man in the heavens could be pretty unforgiving.

"But my mother is a fighter," Fajar continued, "the doctor said that she only had weeks to live, but it's been two months now, and she's still hanging on." Fajar's gaze was lost in the past. He then closed his eyes and took a breath, as if trying to keep his soul from escaping. When he opened his eyes again, Ambar could see tears welling up inside.

"At this point, I know she must be exhausted, Ambar. I just want her to know that I will be okay... because now I have you by my side."

Ambar suddenly felt as if her stomach was filled with rocks.

He thinks that by parading me in front of his dying mother, she can die more peacefully, and he can feel less like a failure to her. Ambar thought. She was unsure if she was interested in being made a Messiah for Fajar and his mother. She realized that she enjoyed spending time with this man simply because he gave her an excuse to avoid being at home with her own queen lioness. On the other hand, she relished the possibility of being the last woman that the queen saw before she passed. After all, she had to pay respect to the previous ruler before she could ascend the throne herself.

It was then that Fajar produced a small bronze box from inside his suit that he hung behind the driver's seat. The sight of the antique-looking item immediately grabbed Ambar's attention. Even under the pale moonlight that shone through the windshield, she could see the intricate snake-like carvings slither through the box's surface. *Traditional Javanese scripts*, Ambar realized. The *hanacaraka.* She remembered her mother had tried to teach her to write and read the letters when she was in elementary school, but she would always find a way to avoid the lessons ("Why should I learn all of this stuff? Even my teacher at school doesn't know how to read this," little Ambar would argue). But if her mother kept pressing, Ambar would make a fuss and cry. She discovered early on that if she cried long enough, her father would eventually swoop in and save her—like the valiant prince that he was—believing that her mother was being too hard on her. Ambar realized that she had always wanted to escape her mother's unwavering and critical gaze for as long as she could remember.

However, Ambar was surprised to find that she could understand the meaning of the ancient texts engraved on the top of the bronze box. It looked and sounded mystical; Ambar swore that it could have been a mantra.

Through my pain and misery,
that was how you came to be.
By the moon and the sun, I swore to thee.
From now to eternity, my heirloom, you'll be.

Ambar saw Fajar open the box's lid and lifted a golden chain necklace with a large green emerald glistening at its end, swarmed by hundreds of white diamonds, making it look like a staring, unblinking eye.

"This belongs to my mother," he said as he laid it on her palm, "and I want you to have it."

Ambar couldn't take her eyes off the gemstone. So arresting yet intimidating its power was that she felt like challenging it.

"Are you sure your mother would want you to give this to me?" Ambar asked, even though she couldn't have cared less.

"Of course," Fajar assured her. "In fact, she specifically asked me to give it to you."

Ambar smiled. She suddenly remembered her father, who had always spoiled her with gifts, from dolls, toys, to a minibike. It didn't matter to her that he had bought those items from a secondhand market by the roadside—every time her father brought something home for her, Ambar felt like a royal daughter.

Fajar wrapped the necklace around Ambar's neck and kissed her forehead. "You look beautiful," he whispered. It was as if Ambar's father had come back to life, making sure that his daughter was treated like the empress that she was.

"Please come to my house with me tomorrow; it would mean so much to me," Fajar said. The way he looked reminded Ambar of a stray kitten begging for scraps, and Ambar could not help but give in.

"Of course I will," Ambar squeezed his hand gently. She could see that her response gave him relief. Locking his gaze with hers, Fajar shifted closer and planted his lips on Ambar's. His hands cupped her face as if he was gulping from it. Ambar pulled her knees onto the seat and rested them on the cushion, driving herself closer, letting him savour the nectar of her lips. He earned every lipstick-tinged drop. After all, he had just invited Ambar to her very own royal coronation—neither wicked stepmother nor fairy godmother necessary. This was better than any fairy tale Ambar could ever dream of.

Scrambling to the back seat, Ambar and Fajar mauled each other as if they lusted for blood. Squirming and writhing like snakes in a cave, they felt freer than ever. Not one drop of light shone on them, and they preferred it that way. Under the shadows, they could be feral animals, not anybody's pets.

Because the light held you captive while the darkness set you free.

What they didn't realize was that a mother's gaze could penetrate through even the darkest of nights. After all, she had seen a glimpse of hell and lived to tell the tale.

So relentlessly unwavering and unflinching were her eyes that shadows folded onto themselves in fear, allowing her a better sight of the abominable act that was splayed on the passenger seat just beyond the rear window.

Her eyes reddened and trembled as she saw her son fornicating with a dishonourable woman.

***

Ambar planted a parting kiss on Fajar's lips before she stepped out of the car several minutes later. Upon alighting on the gravel, she self-consciously pulled at her blouse and skirt, as if afraid that people would know what she had done just by looking at the creases.

Ambar glanced sideways and saw Fajar's car starting up. The beam from the headlight and the rumbling sound from the engine disrupted the quiet night as if alerting every house in the neighborhood that Ambar, the daughter of a pious and God-fearing single mother, was once again being dropped off late at night by a man, like a dirty secret.

As Fajar drove away, Ambar raised her hands to wave at him, hoping to get a wave back or a smile.

However, Ambar could see from the window that Fajar's attention was fixed on the road; his face was devoid of any of the joy that had earlier oozed from his every pore.

He's probably tired. It's after midnight, and we have a big day tomorrow, Ambar reasoned to herself.

But in a split second that followed, Ambar realized that she had seen that look before. It was the look that Fajar had whenever he was alone and thought that nobody was watching.

It was as if his soul was only loaned to him, and someone—or something else—had decided to take it back.

***

"It looks good on you," Fajar complimented Ambar when he saw his mother's necklace encircling her neck.

It was the day after, and Ambar was back in Fajar's car, which looked and smelled the same as it had the night before. However, unlike the gloomy man that Ambar had seen through the window last night, today, Fajar looked as chipper as ever. He kept saying how stunning Ambar was in her long-sleeved white dress and blood-red shoes. Ambar quite liked the look herself as she based it on her favorite fairy tale, Swan Lake, where the prince professed his love and released the princess from her curse, making her a true royal in the end. Her whole ensemble was her way of manifesting her destiny.

However, her mood just couldn't align with her sunny get-up this evening, all thanks to snippy comments made by her mother just before she was about to head out.

"They must pay you a lot of money, don't they?"

Ambar, who was just putting on her crimson shoes, stopped in her tracks and stared at her mother. Her insinuating tone was palpable; she might as well cut Ambar's jugular with a knife.

"Do you know what people in our neighborhood have been talking about?" her mother stood in the living room, a good four feet from where Ambar sat. Wrapped in her oversized black dress, she leaned her shoulder against the wall, her arms folded across her chest as if assessing a shameful object from afar.

Ambar didn't have time for this. She rose from her chair and headed for the front door.

"They said, 'Look at Mrs. Endang's daughter; she's always being taken home late by someone. I wonder what she does for a living'," her mother continued. Rage shook her voice.

As if rotten eggs had just been thrown at her back, Ambar turned to face her aggressor. Her eyes were burning coals.

"I don't give a *fuck* what they think."

The mother hen winced as if Ambar just spat acid on her. *"Have you no shame?"*

The more her mother threw heinous accusations at her, the more she wanted to mess with her mother's head. After all, she had decided that her daughter was a whore. Why bother correcting her now?

"I thought this is what you want, Mother? Me finding a husband? I'm just doing what you told me to."

"Not by disgracing our family in front of everybody!" her mother barked.

"You want to talk about family, Mother? Am I *not* your family?"

Both women breathed heavily; each was a distorted reflection of the other—arch Nemeses bound by blood.

"You are my *daughter*," her mother reminded Ambar's position in this household, "and as your *mother,* it's my duty to guide you through life so you don't do things that you'll regret."

"No, you want me under your thumb," Ambar retorted, "and you think your duty is to point out the things that I lack." Ambar could feel her pent-up anger rolling like a storm.

"When I had to refuse the job offer in Malaysia a couple of years ago because you didn't want to be alone, you belittled me *every day* for not having a job. When I finally got *this* job, you asked me *when* will I have a boyfriend," Ambar's voice cracked, "and now that I have done *exactly* as you asked, *you called me a whore.*"

Her mother just stared at her, dumbfounded, unable to refute Ambar's tirade. Ambar believed there was nothing her mother could do other than admit defeat. But she forgot the fundamental law in this household: Ambar was the *daughter*, and she was the *mother*. And her mother would rather chew on shards of glass than apologize.

"Don't twist my words, Ambar. I have never said such a thing. I'm just telling you what other people have said," her mother's voice trembled, "remember the Quran and the *hadith*, Ambar. Respect and honour your parents. Especially your—."

"You can cite the Quran and the *hadith* all you want, Mother," Ambar snapped, "I'm done feeling guilty for you."

Ambar turned her back on her grief-stricken mother and walked out. In between the sound of her pounding heart, she vowed to move out of her mother's house tonight—never to return.

***

Ambar let her fingers play with the golden necklace on her neck. The gleam of the gemstone at its center shone as brightly as ever, casting specks of light throughout the sprawling living room where she sat.

Ambar marveled at the lavish items and adornments that lay before her eyes. There was a large painting on the wall across from her, stretched from one corner to the next, depicting a traditional shadow puppet show watched by a smattering of locals. Ambar felt as if she was part of them.

As she observed the painting from where she sat, Ambar could see the hand of the puppeteer protruding from behind the white cloth, unnoticed by the rest of the audience. The yellowish glow from the chandelier in the living room made the puppeteer's hands seem to move ever so slightly.

Annoyed by what her mind had conjured up, Ambar shifted her sight to the closed door across the living room, beyond the reach of the chandelier's light. That was where Fajar had disappeared to moments ago. He told Ambar that he wanted to check with the live-in nurse whether his mother was in a good enough condition for a visit. "She seemed well enough this morning. But I better check since her condition fluctuates by the hour."

Ambar glanced at the watch on her wrist—8 p.m. It had been ten minutes since Fajar had left her in the living room, but it felt like hours. She was getting anxious, and knowing that she was sitting there alone, surrounded by antiques and relics with no one else in sight, made her uncomfortable. Determined to shake off her jitters, Ambar rose from the chair and decided to look around.

As she walked across the hall from the living room, her eyes were drawn to her right, where a massive stone carving stretched along the walls. There was a sculpture of a woman wearing a traditional robe, standing in the middle of a forest. She was extending her arms to a sickly-looking old man, offering him a bowl of water. While the woman's eyes brimmed with care and generosity, the old man's visage looked cunning and malicious. It didn't take long for Ambar to realize that she recognized the scene: it was from the Javanese version of the *Ramayana,* the story that her father used to read to her every night.

The woman depicted on the wall was Sita, who, at that particular part of the tale, was tricked by the calculating Rahwana—who disguised himself as an old man—into giving him water. As Sita's arms extended beyond the protective circle made by her prince, the ferocious Rahwana snatched her away and held her hostage in his castle.

The devious glint in Rahwana's eyes sent a shiver down Ambar's spine, yet at the same time, she couldn't look away. The frail man on the wall, with his apparent harmlessness, drew her in, just like he did poor Sita.

Ambar thought that it was understandable why Sita didn't suspect the man's true intention. Carved in broad, expressive strokes, the old man seemed to have the most friendly laugh. She couldn't only identify with Sita, but also feared for her. Ambar realized that she had also been drawn by that very laugh many weeks ago when she thought that her humour was too grim for most people.

"Yes, Mother..."

A voice as thin as air jolted Ambar out of her thoughts. Her gaze immediately swerved to where she believed the voice was coming from.

The closed black door.

Thinking that Fajar would emerge from behind the door and invite her in at any moment, Ambar made a last-minute attempt to smooth out her hair and dress. After all, she only had one chance to impress the dying queen.

However, after minutes passed without any sign of the black door opening, Ambar began to feel annoyed.

How hard is it for him to ask whether his mother is in good enough condition for a visit? Ambar thought impatiently. Surely the nurse can give him a quick answer?

Ambar's questions floated aimlessly in the air without any answers to keep them earthbound. She turned her head to the living room, contemplating whether to just return there and wait like an uncomplaining little girl, when she, once again, saw a glimpse of the *Ramayana* carvings across the wall. The scheming Rahwana now seemed to be laughing *at her*.

Ambar quickly turned her sight back to the coal-black door. There was no way that she would spend another minute waiting there under the encroaching gaze of those relics.

Ambar drew a deep breath. She knew that she just had to walk through the door and ask nicely whether there was something she could do to help. After all, she was Fajar's secretary.

As she clasped her hand on the door handle, she could see a faint red gleam cast onto the door's surface. She noticed that it came from the gemstone in her necklace. *Has it always been red?* Ambar didn't care enough to remember, as her focus was to make sure she made an impressive entrance.

The door was heavier than she had anticipated when Ambar pushed it open. A long creaking sound filled the air as the door swung inwards, revealing—to Ambar's surprise—not a well-lit bedroom fit for a queen but a dark cavern.

Ambar stood, statue-like, in the doorway, trying to adjust her eyes to the gaping darkness in front of her. There were cobbled stairs ahead, leading down to an even darker abyss. She was about to call out Fajar's name, but something in her head told her not to. She knew something was wrong, but she didn't want to turn back before getting some answers. She needed to find Fajar and asked him what the hell was going on. And if she had to walk down that flight of stairs to get her answers, so be it.

Ambar took out her cellphone from her handbag and turned on the flashlight app. The white beam emanating from the device gave her enough sense of what lay ahead. Unfortunately, the light was still too weak to reveal what was in store for her at the end of the pit.

Ambar inhaled deeply before started descending the cobblestone stairs. She could feel the door behind her being swung shut by the wind, engulfing her in suffocating darkness.

As she treaded deeper into the womb of the cavern, Ambar was greeted by a chilling breeze—and with it, a distant but unmistakable voice.

"I'll fetch her, Mother."

It was Fajar's voice, which sounded both adoring and fearful. Every word he said bounced off the stone wall into Ambar's ears, creating an overlapping squawk that looped endlessly.

"I'll I'll fetch fetch her her, Mother Mother.
I'll I'll fetch fetch her her, Mother Mother.
I'll I'll fetch fetch her her, Mother Mother."

Ambar stopped in her tracks, realizing that she was almost at the foot of the stairs. In front of her was a landing that led to a low archway on the right, where Fajar's voice resounded.

The hair on Ambar's neck stood up when she heard the sound of the walls breathing, resulting in a cacophony of whispery chants from hell. Only moments later did she realize that the panting sound was coming from her own mouth.

"You wait here, Mother. I'll be right back," Fajar's voice continued to undulate in the darkness, but now it sounded closer than before.

Ambar's heart sank when she saw a man's shadow appear on the cobbled floor, approaching the mouth of the archway. Fajar was coming for her.

Ambar turned back to the stairs and started climbing to the black door. At this moment, she wanted nothing more than to make her legs move faster, but the blinding darkness and her godforsaken stiletto heels made her attempt at running more like a light jog than a dash.

Ambar screamed in frustration as she hobbled her way towards the upper landing, where the black door was. Her escape was now in sight. A few more steps and she would be able to ditch her shoes and sprint as fast as she could—or fight.

"Ambaaaaar!" Fajar's bestial roar followed her from several steps below. The thumping of his feet sounded more and more frantic as he got closer.

Skipping over the last two steps, Ambar reached the upper landing and swung open the obsidian door. Without even blinking to adjust her eyes to the piercing light, she kicked off her crimson shoes and ran for her life.

As she ran past the living room where Rahwana's smile taunted her from the wall, Ambar felt a tightening grip around her neck. Thinking that she must be hyperventilating, she desperately pleaded for her lungs to hold on just a little longer. The main front door was right there in front of her, ready to grant her an escape. All she had to do was pay no mind to her heaving lungs and aching body and keep pushing. She was sure that she would be out in the front yard in no time, free to scream and yell to anyone who would listen.

But the tightness around her neck intensified the closer she got to the front door. Now, barely an iota of air could enter her lungs. Ambar's run regressed into a blundering shamble. Her mouth agape, she gasped for air. As her fingers clawed violently at her neck, she felt chain loops coil tightly around her throat. She wasn't hyperventilating; she was being strangled by her own necklace.

Ambar's body slumped to the floor. Devoid of oxygen, her head felt like it would topple to the ground. The front door, which before had looked ridiculously near, now seemed miles away.

From behind, she could hear Fajar's footsteps approaching, steady and triumphant, eager to claim his prey.

"It will choke you to death if you keep running away," Fajar spoke calmly as if he was explaining the laws of physics. Ambar could feel Fajar's hand resting on her shoulders. He then pulled her backward, letting her rest in his arms as he knelt.

"I need your body to be well, Ambar. It's the only way I can have my mom back," Fajar said; his tone was as loving as ever, "but you don't need to be scared. Everything's going to be all right. I promise you. You won't feel a thing."

That was the last thing Ambar heard before her whole world turned black.

***

At least Fajar kept part of his promise. Minutes later, when Ambar regained consciousness, she didn't feel any pain. She found herself sitting on a chair in a dingy chamber. The only light source in the room was a chain bulb that hung from the ceiling. Ambar could taste the pungent smell of rats' droppings that permeated the air, making her gag. Tears, snot, and spit dripped down her face like melting wax, wreaking havoc with her make-up.

As she examined her own situation, Ambar could see that her hands were lying idly on her thigh, and her bare feet were resting on the cold stone floor. There was no rope tying her to the chair. Nothing that could keep her from fighting back and making a run for it. However, when she tried to lift her hands, it was as if there were iron cuffs that held them in place. Her feet, too, felt like they were weighed down by a heavy-duty ball and chain.

As her eyes darted in panic, trying to make sense of what was happening, she caught the sight of the necklace with a dangling emerald eye on its end, still coiling around her neck like a greedy snake. The previously green gemstone that formed its pupil now took on a reddish hue, making it look like a gaping, throbbing wound. Recalling what had occurred minutes ago when she tried to escape, Ambar suspected that, as unbelievable as it might sound, this life-like necklace was somehow responsible for her currently paralyzed state.

"Hi," seemingly out of nowhere, Fajar's face filled her whole view. Ambar opened her mouth to scream, but no sound came out. She was as silent and defenseless as a carcass.

Fajar kept staring at her for a moment. So close was his face to hers that Ambar could see every bead of sweat leaking from the pores of his skin.

"You're fine. You're not hurt," Fajar cupped Ambar's tear-stained face and moved it around in his hands as if checking for a defect. There was a worried glint in his eyes; Ambar was unsure whether his remark was supposed to soothe her or himself.

"I love you, Ambar," Fajar whispered as he caressed Ambar's trembling face, "and I love my mother. I need to have you both."

Ambar stared at Fajar in confusion. But as he moved away from her sight, Ambar was able to look ahead and got her answer. What she saw in front of her made her eyes bulge in fear.

Sitting right across from her were skeletal remains of a human, covered in filth and dirt. Its big hollow eyes were emotionless and bare, while its lipless mouth was forever grinning. Ambar couldn't comprehend how something devoid of a soul could look so cunning.

"That horrible disease took her months ago," Fajar lamented as he rested his hands on the bony shoulder of what once was his mother's, "before she died, she promised that she would always be with me... that she would always watch over me."

Fajar's voice cracked as emotions overtook him, "But I don't want just her *presence* or her *memory.* I want her *here*. I want her *alive*, healthy, and well."

"And then I met you," the man smiled that deceptively warm smile, "you're fierce, funny, and intelligent, just like she was. Right then, I knew...."

Fajar's voice petered out as if losing its transmitter. Ambar could see his hands move to his mother's collarbone, where a familiar object lay bare and loose: the emerald necklace, identical to the one twisting around her own neck.

"I knew that you two would get along. Two of my favorite women, in the same body."

Ambar managed to let out a muffled scream. Her whole body jerked and trembled, trying to free herself from the spell that rendered her immobile. But those invisible chains just would not give.

Fajar turned his attention to the dark corner of the room and said giddily, "Isn't she perfect, Mother?"

With growing horror, Ambar's eyes followed his gaze to the shadowy wall. There was only a deep blackness there. But Fajar kept going.

"Did I do right by you, Mother?" Fajar, ever the approval-seeking man-boy, clung to the dead woman who was pulling his strings.

Trying to make sense of it all, Ambar stared deep into the dark corner of the wall, searching for something that wasn't there. The more she frowned, the more she felt like darkness was closing in on her, forcing her to look deeper.

And then she saw her, hiding behind the ink-black shadows. The queen of the house. Her face was as pale as the moonlight. Her body looked frail and spindly, as if the disease was still eating her away, even after she died. But there was something burning in her eyes. An untamed desire to protect what was hers. Ambar knew those eyes well. She had tried to escape those eyes all her life. They were the eyes of a mother.

Ambar could only scream and wail in silence. In the moments before darkness engulfed her, Ambar prayed that her mother could think of her, forgive her, and eventually look for her.

It was then that Fajar began to recite a passage that sounded familiar to Ambar. Every word seemed to multiply and gnaw over one another like rats, burrowing a chamber into her mind. So ethereal and mystical were those verses; she could swear they could have been a mantra.

"Through my pain and misery,
that was how you came to be.
By the moon and the sun, I swore to thee.
From now to eternity, my heirloom, you'll be."

LARAS AND THE DWELLER OF THE HOUSE

Laras buried her fingers deep into her palm with all her might. She prayed that her fingernails would carve gaping holes in her skin so that her fear could emerge through it like a genie from a lamp.

"What are you doing?"

Irma's rebuke from the driver's seat made Laras hide her hands immediately inside the pockets of her red school skirt like a thief. All Laras' fears were now not only trapped under her skin but also crawled through her insides like centipedes.

"Nothing, Mama," the tickling legs of the centipedes on her bones made her shudder.

"If I see another scar on your hand, you're not sleeping in your room tonight. You hear me?"

Laras looked at her mother, confused. "Are we not staying at Uti[33]'s house tonight?"

"You got grades like this, and you're still hoping to stay at Uti's house?" Irma's sharp retort pierced Laras' ear, causing her to shift towards the door.

---

[33] Short for *Eyang Putri,* a kinship term used to address grandmother in the Javanese language.

Laras was about to protest, but nine years of living with her mother had taught her to stay quiet, even though her tongue was constantly twisting like an eel caught in a net. In her head, Laras recalled the words from Mrs. Jenar, her homeroom teacher, half an hour before, when the middle-aged woman had handed Laras' report card to her mother at school.

"Laras' grades are declining this semester," Mrs. Jenar said. Sitting next to her mother, Laras felt like Mrs. Jenar had just kicked her into the sea. She wanted to ask why Mrs. Jenar chose to tell her mother about Laras' declining grades first rather than her achievements.

Laras remembered that she had won 2nd place in the children's violin competition at school last month after competing with older participants who were all 5th and 6th graders. Laras also knew that she had been getting the highest marks in her English class for two semesters in a row. She couldn't comprehend why Mrs. Jenar didn't remind her mother about all these things.

"Laras needs to improve her grades in Mandarin, Mathematics, and Physical Education if she wants her overall score ranking to go up," Mrs. Jenar showed Laras and her mother a list of grades printed on the report card. Laras could see the three B marks blazing there, forcing all eyes—primarily her mother's—to focus solely on them. Even though the A marks dominated Laras' report card, her mother's expression made it clear that Laras shouldn't feel content about any of this.

As if able to intercept Laras' memories, her mother barked again, yanking Laras back to the present, where she sat nervously in the moving car. "When I bought you the iPad last month, what did you promise me?"

That my grades would remain good, Laras was about to answer, but her tongue wriggled beyond her control and instead replied, "Maybe if I didn't have to take violin, ballet, and abacus lessons, I could've had time to study."

Laras' heart seemed to stop beating for a moment when she realized what she just had said. Her mother's face turned furious as if she had just been spat on. Laras' body swayed violently as the SUV turned sharply to the left and pulled over by the roadside, a few kilometers away from their house. Laras knew she was in big trouble.

With her back pressed against the passenger door, Laras watched her mother stare. The matriarch didn't say anything for a few moments, but her gaze was sharp with rebukes. Laras would have preferred her mother to just yell or lash out—anything other than staring at her like a predator.

After a few minutes, Laras lowered her eyes, yielding to her mother's overpowering gaze. Her fingers twirled the hem of her school uniform nervously. Only then did she hear her mother speak.

"Just quit school altogether then," Irma taunted. "You feel like you've had enough studying, right?"

Laras felt her mind go blank. She couldn't understand how her mother could have arrived at that conclusion from what she had said.

Laras' face heated up. She wanted to follow the overwhelming urge to scream and thrash like a feral animal. But Laras knew that rebelling would only lead to more severe punishment. She shuddered as she recalled the dark storeroom on the second floor of her house, where she had spent several nights due to declining grades, forgetting to practice reading the Quran and *hadith*, or a lousy violin practice session with her mother. She knew something was hiding behind the room's worn-out boxes and metal shelves. Laras was sure of it because every time she spent the night there, she always saw a pair of eyes lurking from the dark corner of the storeroom where the ends of the two shelves almost met. The irises of the eyes were white, but instead of glowing, they looked dull and old. Laras remembered chanting a prayer while weeping the last time she had spent the night there, but instead of running away, those eyes stayed put as if basking in her prayer.

At a loss for how else to behave, Laras let her tears flow down her cheeks.

"Now, why are you crying? I thought that's what you want. No need to go to school, no need to take lessons... You already got a lot of 'A's anyway," her mother continued to mock, making Laras' tears stream down as if from a running faucet. A few moments later, Laras heard the words that she had been dreading.

"You're sleeping in the storeroom tonight."

Laras' heart froze. The thought of going back to spend the night in that stuffy room, encircled by darkness, made her sob even louder. For a moment, Laras' thoughts brought her back to the storeroom. She remembered the strange odour that hung in the musty air. At first, it smelled like jasmines in her grandparents' yard. But there was also a hint of another scent underneath it that made her shudder—a rancid smell, like something that had been dead for a long time. Laras was sure that the pungent smell came from the white-eyed creature that dwelled there.

Laras could see that her mother was about to continue her tirade when a sudden knock on the driver's window made her stop and turn around.

Outside the window was a stout, dark-skinned, middle-aged woman with her hair curled behind her head. The woman gave a smile that Irma and Laras knew very well, a smile meant to calm Irma whenever she scolded Laras. Irma pushed the button on the side of the driver's door and let the side window slide down.

"Sumi?" Irma said, glancing at the green shopping bag in Sumi's hand. "Why are you going shopping now at this time of night?"

"I'm sorry, Mbak Irma," Sumi said softly, as she usually did when talking to Irma. "This morning after you left, I went to the convenience store to buy the oxtail meat, but they were out of it. They said it would be restocked this evening. That's why I'm on my way there again."

"You should've checked with other places too this morning, Sumi. An oxtail soup takes a long time to cook. When will we have dinner if you just bought the meat now?"

Even though Irma's voice rose, there wasn't the slightest look of panic on Sumi's face. Years of working as a housekeeper at Irma's house had made her adept at dealing with every spike of anger, which was often triggered by the slightest error.

"There's a way to cook oxtail meat so that it becomes tender in only half an hour," Sumi assured Irma. "I found it on the internet." She glanced at Laras, sitting with her head down in the passenger seat, before asking in a cheerful tone.

"Mbak Laras, how are your grades?"

"Her grades are declining. That's why I'm having a word with her. We won't be staying over at Mom's house tonight."

"Oh, I see… That means Mbak Laras has to study harder then. I hope it's okay if I join in, so I can learn a thing or two," Sumi joked.

Laras cast a helpless look at Sumi. She thought how nice it would be to be outside the car like Mbak Sumi at this very moment, where she would be able to walk away from her mother at any time, go to the convenience store, or do anything, as long as she could delay her return home—or even not go home at all. The noisy, dusty street full of speeding vehicles under the darkening sky felt safer for her.

As if she could read Laras' thoughts, Sumi said, "Mbak Laras, do you want to go shopping with me?"

Laras' heart immediately somersaulted at the invitation as if she had been struck by lightning. Mbak Sumi had just opened the door for her, but, of course, her freedom hinged on her mother's generosity, which she knew was currently in short supply. Laras looked at her mother, bracing herself for a rejection.

"Well, do you want to go shopping with Mbak Sumi or not?" Her mother swiftly turned to her, "If you don't want to, we'll go straight home right now."

"I want to go with Mbak Sumi!" Laras squealed a little too quickly. She immediately opened the door and jumped out of the car. The bottom part of her school uniform dangled outside her red skirt and was full of wrinkles—something that would surely be the source of another reprimand. But this time, Laras didn't care. Even just stepping out of the car made her feel that she was in a completely different world—a more joyful one.

Laras stood by the pavement, waiting for Mbak Sumi to walk over. Pleasure ran through her whole body, making it hard for her to stand still.

"Don't take too long, okay, Sumi. Go straight home afterward," Laras heard her mother say. Shortly after, Laras saw the passenger window of the car slide down, revealing her mother's glaring eyes, boring right into her soul.

"Don't ask Mbak Sumi to do other things other than shopping. It's late. You know what happens to children who roam outside at dusk, right?"

"They are kidnapped by the *Jinns*," Laras replied dutifully, to the approving nod of her mother. Even though the story of the shape-shifting spirits who snatch children after dark used to give her night terrors, there was nothing more nightmarish for Laras at that moment than her mother's glare.

As soon as her mother's car was out of sight, Laras inched forward and hugged Mbak Sumi. Her head rested on the woman's bloated stomach, holding her tightly before she burst into an agonizing cry. Between her sobs, Laras could smell a mildly sweet scent emanating from Mbak Sumi's skin, making Laras want to bury herself even deeper in Mbak Sumi's embrace.

Mbak Sumi slowly let go of Laras' arms and crouched down to meet Laras' eyes, which now seemed to gleam like crystal.

"I don't want to go home, Mbak Sumi," Laras' face was red, desperately holding back her sobs, "Mama said, I have to sleep in the storeroom again tonight."

"She probably just said that because she was still upset. Give her a moment, and you'll see that everything will be back to normal."

Lara shook her head, "Mama's angry because I asked for my courses to be reduced, and then Mama said I don't have to go to school anymore." Laras cried again.

Sumi put her hands on Laras cheeks and wiped her tears. "Okay, how about this: if she still asks you to sleep in the storeroom tonight, I'll accompany you there, so you don't have to worry anymore. Deal?"

The knowledge that she wouldn't have to face the darkness in the storeroom alone tonight made Laras' heart sigh with relief. Her sobs slowly subsided. Mbak Sumi gave her a proud smile as if Laras had just won a math contest. Laras realized that she had never seen a smile like that from her own mother.

Walking side by side towards the convenience store under the darkened sky, Mbak Sumi and Laras used their time to talk about whatever was on their minds, although Mbak Sumi assumed the role of the listener most of the time.

"If Mama finds out you're sleeping in the store-room with me, won't that get you in trouble?" Laras asked. She had often seen her mother scold Mbak Sumi for various things: from a few missing or damaged clothes, floors that hadn't been mopped, to food that had secretly been laced with artificial flavor enhanc-ers—which her mother hated. Every time Laras' mother reprimanded Mbak Sumi, the sound of her screeching sent a shiver down Laras' spine. Even so, Mbak Sumi had never looked upset. She responded to each re-proach with merely a nod and a kind voice, as if harsh words could no longer hurt her.

Seeing how often Mbak Sumi was scolded by her mother for the same mistakes, Laras began to suspect that maybe Mbak Sumi had been making these mistakes on purpose. Laras realized that she herself was doing the same thing. Laras, for example, wouldn't study or do homework if her mother wasn't at home to either supervise or yell at her. Instead, she would spend time watching television and running around the house, no matter how often her mother reprimanded her afterwards.

Perhaps that's the only thing that makes us happy, Laras thought. Laras only hoped that Mbak Sumi had never thought of putting anything in her cooking that would make Laras and her mother sick. Or worse.

"I would probably get reprimanded a little, but then, as usual, everything would be back to normal," Mbak Sumi replied casually. "Besides, your Mom would definitely be overwhelmed if she didn't have me around."

Laras was amused at the thought of her mother being overwhelmed with house chores without Mbak Sumi's help. But her laughter subsided when she realized that she couldn't even imagine what would happen if Mbak Sumi wasn't with them.

"Mbak Sumi?" Laras called out amid her steps on the cobbled pavement.

"Yes, Mbak Laras?"

"You'll continue working at our house, right?"

Laras saw a warm smile spread on Mbak Sumi's face, "As long as I'm healthy and capable, I'll definitely keep working for your Mom. That's why I pray that I'll always be blessed with good health."

Mbak Sumi's answer didn't calm Laras' nerves. She realized that Mbak Sumi couldn't possibly work for her mother forever. As time went by, Mbak Sumi would get older. Her body would get progressively weaker. Laras' gaze turned to Mbak Sumi's feet which were encased in a pair of worn-down flip-flops. Stretching from her dull yellow skirt that hung down to her calf, Mbak Sumi's left leg looked swollen. The skin under her ankles seemed to swell up as if a giant clam had lodged itself underneath it. Laras realized that Mbak Sumi's steps were a little wobbly. Gradually, her fears returned.

What if Mbak Sumi is suddenly no longer able to work? Surely she'll have to return to her village and leave me alone with Mama.

Laras' eyes caught sight of a boy her age, standing side by side with his father on the side of the road. They were watching the banana fritter vendor preparing their orders on his food stall. Seeing them spending the afternoon together made Laras' heart throb with envy.

All of this would be different if Papa were still at home, she thought.

Laras wasn't sure if she should say what she had been thinking to Mbak Sumi, but the words were prickling her tongue. She decided to blurt it out anyway, "Mbak Sumi, what's Papa like?"

Laras knew that her question surprised Mbak Sumi. It took a while before she could answer.

"Oh, he's very kind and patient. And he really loves you."

"If he loves me, why doesn't he ever visit me?" Laras asked, even though she already knew the answer. Her mother had forbidden her father to contact Laras for years, ever since he left home when she was only three years old. Laras had heard a heated argument between her mother and her grandparents some time ago after they suggested that her mother allow Laras to communicate with her father.

"She has the right to meet her father," Laras heard Uti say to her mother the last time they visited her grandparents. At that time, Laras was listening to the music in the family room, not far from the kitchen where they were talking. Her earphones didn't actually play anything from her iPad. Laras just really wanted to hear what was being discussed.

"Mom, please don't tell me how to raise my daughter. I never vilified you for how you raised me, did I?"

Her mother's snappy response seemed to have offended her grandmother, "Tell me then. How do you think I have raised you? Did I ever teach you to be rude to your husband? Did I ever teach you to just give up whenever there's a problem in your marriage?"

"You don't even know what I went through with him!" her mother exploded.

What happened next was a familiar screaming match. Like a TV show that she had seen repeatedly, Laras could predict when Akung[34] would come and lead his daughter into the guest room so that she could calm herself down. Shortly after, the atmosphere in the house would become unbearably quiet. But Laras could always hear Akung's soothing whispers to her mother from the guest room. A few hours later, Laras' mother would walk out of the guest room and immediately take Laras home.

"When it comes to this, I think you should ask your Mom when she's in a good mood," Mbak Sumi replied, bringing Laras' mind back to the present.

"She's never in a good mood," Laras grumbled spontaneously, which was greeted with amused laugh-

---

[34] Short for *Eyang Kakung,* a kinship term used to address grandfather in the Javanese language.

ter from Mbak Sumi. Laras giggled too. She found it strangely liberating to find something funny in an unfortunate situation.

Laras could see the convenience store they were going to. The colourful signage shone brightly, eclipsing the moonlight in the night sky. Laras' face lit up at the sight of the colours and the noise from the nearby crowd. However, at the same time, Laras also understood what it meant: Her curfew was approaching.

The heck with it, Laras thought bitterly. It doesn't matter whether I get home on time. I'll still have to sleep in the storeroom tonight anyway—and I'll have Mbak Sumi there beside me.

"You just have to pray so that Allah will bless your Mom with more patience and understanding," Mbak Sumi said.

"When I slept in the storeroom a few days ago, I did pray, but I didn't pray for her," Laras admitted, "I prayed that I could live with Papa or you."

Laras thought that Mbak Sumi would react happily to this, but, to her disappointment, Mbak Sumi just kept on walking.

Would she not feel happy if I lived with her? Laras suddenly felt sad.

"I'll always wish you the very best," Mbak Sumi finally said.

Those words evoked something that had been troubling Laras' mind. She stopped in her tracks and called out, "Mbak Sumi?"

Mbak Sumi, who was already a few steps ahead, turned her head as soon as she realized that Laras was no longer by her side. As she walked back to Laras, she asked, "What's the matter?"

"Does Allah truly listen to our prayers?"

"Why do you ask that?"

Laras didn't know how to answer. Her head was filled with memories that caught her breath and made her heart race. Laras remembered how scared she was every time she practiced the violin with her mother. Every wrong note would trigger a rebuke, making Laras more nervous and clumsy. She also remembered the revision nights with her mother, how her mother would shout at Laras after every wrong answer to her mother's quiz. She also recalled her mother's anger whenever she misread the Arabic script in the Quran and *hadith*.

Every second, Laras prayed that she would be able to strike the violin's strings properly, even though her fingers were shaking. She prayed that she would be able to answer all her mother's quizzes during revision nights. She also prayed that she could read Arabic scripts in the Quran and *hadith* correctly.

But above all, Laras prayed that someone could take her away from her mother.

But no one came. Not her father, not her grandparents. Even Mbak Sumi could only give reassuring words and not much else.

"Maybe God doesn't love me," Laras' voice cracked. She sobbed, "Papa doesn't love me either."

Mbak Sumi once again crouched on the pavement in front of Laras. The tears that flooded Laras' eyes reduced the passing cars on the road into a series of rippling lights and images. It was only Mbak Sumi's face in front of her that kept its shape—the only real thing that she could hold on to. But Laras could see Mbak Sumi's face twitched as she moved closer. There was something beneath her skin that snaked up to the surface. At first, Laras thought that Mbak Sumi was about to cry. Only then did Laras realize that Mbak Sumi's face looked too heated to shed tears.

Mbak Sumi wrapped her arms around Laras. Immediately, Laras rested her head on Mbak Sumi's shoulder, hoping to find comfort in the warmth of her skin. But she was surprised to feel a piercing coldness emanating from it like a sheet of ice. Laras also noticed that the sweet scent that had previously radiated from Mbak Sumi's body was slowly drifting away, like a perfume that had started to lose its charm. What was left was a familiar scent that made Laras' hair stand up on the back of her neck.

It was the sour smell of something old and mouldy.

The smell of the figure in the storeroom.

Laras' whole body shivered. Right away, she knew something was wrong. Laras had known Mbak Sumi all her life. When Laras was younger, Mbak Sumi had often fed and bathed her, but Laras had never once smelled this pungent scent from her body.

With her hands still clinging to Mbak Sumi, Laras lifted her head. She realized that she could no longer hear the noises from the street. There was no visible puff of smoke from the vehicles or street vendors that had previously filled the air. When Laras' eyes focused, looking at everything surrounding her, her chest suddenly tightened.

She was no longer on the sidewalk to the convenience store. There was no colourful signage shining as bright as the moonlight. What lay before her eyes now was an empty road that snaked forward and disappeared beneath the horizon. The sky that unfolded before her now seemed to have been painted with soot. The only light source in that place was a pair of twin moons floating in the sky.

No, they aren't moons, Laras realized when she saw the two white spheres glided and flicker. *They are eyes.*

"Mbak Sumi…" Laras called softly even though she knew it wasn't Mbak Sumi who held her in an embrace. An ancient voice, which burrowed through Laras' ears, said it all.

"*She can't protect you, my child,*" the creature whispered, taking off all its disguises. "*No one loves you as much I do.*"

There was no trace of Mbak Sumi's warm voice left in there. What resonated in Laras' ears now was a crackle of flame. The creature's body, which had previously been wrapped in Mbak Sumi's dull yellow house dress, was now covered with a long white cloth hanging from its shoulders to the ground. The human skin that had before hidden its true form was now as hard as wood.

Laras cried in fear. She tried to free herself from the creature's embrace, but the cold, bony hands gripped her tighter and lifted her off the ground. Her sobs grew louder, turning into a heartbreaking wail that tore up the night. The figure began to rock her gently as if tending to its own child.

"There's no need to be afraid, my child," the dry voice whispered, "I'm the one who hears your prayers. I love you more than the man in the sky."

Laras could feel the figure's long fingers slip through her hair. Something in its strokes made Laras' eyelids feel heavy. Slowly her head lowered again, lulled by a gentle touch from the dweller of darkness. She knew she would be drifting off into oblivion in a few moments—if she wasn't there already.

A moment before she fell asleep into the arms of the night, Laras recalled one particular *hadith* that she had read during one of the study sessions with her mother. She remembered how it had first made her afraid of the dark. But it was only now she realized that it was the darkness that had been listening to her cries all along.

"Cover your utensils and tie your water skins, and close your doors and keep your children close to you at night, as the Jinns spread out at such time and snatch things away." (Shahih al-Bukhari 3316, Book 59, Hadith 122)

UP THE COTTONWOOD TREE

"Mrs. Surani?" Siti entered the bedroom, where the old woman rested her back against the headboard. There was a large two-pane window next to her bed, framed by red linen curtains open on each side. Through the window, a pale moon floated above the lawn, casting its faint beam over a big old tree outside.

Siti sat next to Mrs. Surani on the bed and said, "I'm sorry, Ma'am, but your medicine ran out. I have looked in the medicine cabinets in the other rooms but I couldn't find any of the medicine left. But maybe this can help?" Siti handed Mrs. Surani a strip of over-the-counter paracetamols that she had brought from home.

As soon as she saw those white tablets, Mrs. Surani spoke softly in between breaths, "They won't do, dear."

Siti nodded, trying to maintain her calm. She might not be a nurse, but she knew that showing panic or cluelessness would only make everything worse.

The only medicine that will work on her is that liquid in the bottle. Siti remembered what Mrs. Surani's husband, Mr. Jamuri, told her when she first arrived at this house weeks ago. Which was why, Siti figured, Mrs. Surani's husband had to travel all the way to the neighbouring village to get that specific medicine from a particular healer, while Siti was tasked to take care of Mrs. Surani for the night.

Making sure she was helping the best she could, Siti asked, "Is there anything else that I can get you to help with your headache, Ma'am?"

The old lady managed a smile, even though Siti knew she was in pain. The earnestness that emanated from the woman's gaze reminded Siti of her late mother, near the end of her life. There was a loving and maternal aura to Mrs. Surani that made Siti immediately feel safe in taking on the job, even though the place was hours away from her own home.

"I am fine now, my dear. It's going away at the moment," she spoke softly, and then chuckled, "I swear this headache is just like a newborn baby: sleeps through the day and awake through the night."

Siti noticed that the woman was about to say something more, but hesitated before finally saying, with feigned lightness, "Well, not that I ever had a child."

Not knowing how to respond, Siti turned her attention to the sheet that covered the entire bed. She could see Mrs. Surani's long, loose hair spread out on the soft surface. Its obsidian colour seemed to deepen under the gloomy light. Siti remembered her own mother used to have flowing hair like this before that horrible disease wilted it away. The thought of it made her heart ache.

"Why do you look sad, my dear?" Mrs. Surani's voice broke her reverie.

Siti stammered, "Who, me? No, I was just thinking about… about…"

Mrs. Surani reached to Siti's hands, as if consoling her, "You know when I was young, my parents always said, '*Surani, don't frown or you'll scare off boys!*' Mind you, I do look like I could eat people when I frown. It didn't help that my hair back then looked like a banyan tree."

Both women let out a hearty laugh. There was a spark of good-natured playfulness when she remarked, "You must drive the boys crazy. You're pretty, kind, smart, and young—how old are you again?"

"I'm twenty-three," Siti replied, greeted by a humorous act of self-pity by Mrs. Surani.

"Twenty-three!" she exclaimed, "now, why did you choose to spend the night with an old woman like me in the middle of nowhere? Your boyfriend must've been really upset!"

Siti laughed, "I don't have a boyfriend, Ma'am. I would much rather be here making myself useful than going on dates pretending to have a good time."

Mrs. Surani emitted a laugh as she clasped Siti's hand in an act of support, "Well, I know that a good man will come eventually for you, and by then you will never have to pretend anymore, and—"

Mrs. Surani stopped herself as her eyes caught the purplish mark on Siti's lower arm which the young woman had been trying to hide with her long-sleeve shirt. "Oh, that looks painful. How did you get these bruises, dear?"

Siti pulled her arms away from Mrs. Surani as if having been scalded by a flame. "Iron deficiency, Ma'am," she contended. From Mrs. Surani's gaze, Siti knew that the old woman was not convinced.

Intrusive ringing from the landline outside granted Siti her escape from the conversation. She saw the concern on Mrs. Surani face reverting back to the pained look that she showed earlier that night. It was clear to Siti that the headache had returned. She asked if the woman needed anything to help with the pain, but

Mrs Surani assured her that the pain would go away in a minute, just like before. "You can get the phone, my dear. It might be something important."

Siti exited the master bedroom and walked towards the ringing landline on the table. She knew it was her housemate, Indun, who was calling. About an hour before, after finding out that there was no medicine left at the house, Siti phoned Indun in panic to ask for advice. There was nothing that Indun could do, of course, other than calming Siti's nerves, but she promised to check on Siti in a few minutes and here she was.

But, when Siti raised the receiver to her ear, it was not Indun's voice that she heard.

It was a man's voice: the one that she knew so well.

"Now listen you little cunt. If you don't come back here this instance, I'll come there and drag you by the hair. Do you understand?"

Siti slammed the phone to the cradle as if those words burned her. She knew that it was only a matter of time before her husband found out where she was, but she didn't expect it to be this soon; it had only been three weeks since she ran away.

Suddenly feeling dizzy, Siti rested her hands against the table for support. She considered taking the handset off the hook to stop the man from calling again but it was too late as the phone reverberated its deafening chime throughout the house, assailing her.

Siti was tempted to leave it ringing in hoping that the caller would tire himself, but the simultaneous sound of Mrs. Surani's moaning in pain in the master bedroom made Siti feel as if she could faint. Siti decided to pick the phone up and be done with it. "Don't ever call here again or I'll call the police."

"Siti? It's me."

A much kinder voice. It was Indun's. With a concerned tone, she asked if everything was okay. Desperately trying to steady her breath, Siti responded, "Yes, I'm fine, Indun. It was just a wrong number."

"At this hour?" Indun sounded doubtful, "Are you sure?"

Siti pondered for a second before sighing, tired and defeated, "Padil just called me, 'Ndun."

There was silence from the other end. Siti could imagine that her friend was also in shock. But, strangely enough, in the minutes that had passed, Siti had started to accept that this was inevitable—even though her acknowledging it did not make Padil's sudden call any less crushing.

"He said he will come here and drag me back if I don't come home," Siti reiterated that awful threat. As much as she tried to suppress her emotions, they kept clawing up and choking her throat. Her bleary eyes gazed at the bruises on her arm, which seemed as fresh and painful as when Padil punched her there three weeks ago. A quiet resolve slowly emerged within her.

"He knows where I am 'Ndun. I don't think I can stay here anymore."

As with any person on the run, Siti had a backup plan. She knew that running away from her house and living with her best friend in a newly rented house was not going to be her endgame. She knew she had to think two steps ahead of her hunter and disappear before he could find her. She knew she had to survive.

Weeks before, she had told Indun that she had decided to take the job to take care of Mrs. Surani. She figured that the job would be simple enough. Take care of Mrs Surani while her husband goes off to work, nine hours a day, five days a week. Which Siti had been doing for almost three weeks now.

However, the first time Siti told her friend of the location where her work would take place, Indun argued that it would be a waste of time since the location was deep in a remote village, hours away from where they lived. "Instead of wasting hours of your time on the road, you could just work at the convenience store here. It is practically next door to our house," Indun reasoned over dinner.

At that time, Siti did not want to argue with her friend. She remembered, in hoping to stall the impending argument, she chose to clear the dining table and brought all of the dishes to the sink. But Indun continued on: "If it's because of the money, we can figure something out, 'Ti," she assured. "I'm just worried. That place is quite far from here and you don't know anyone there. What if you need urgent help? I cannot just will myself to be there instantly, as much as I want to."

Siti was about to turn on the tap over the sink—just to show Indun that she was not interested in the conversation anymore—but then she thought better of it and turned to her friend.

"I think you know *why* I have to do this, 'Ndun," she said sternly, "this is the only way I can get enough money fast, so I can be as far away from him as possible."

Indun threw in a short response as her last attempt at talking some sense into her friend, "I don't know if you notice but Jakarta is a *very* well-known place, 'Ti."

"And it's a *very* big place as well," Siti retorted.

Indun let out a heavy sigh, defeated at last. Deep down she knew that she would not be able to change

Siti's mind whenever that girl had put her mind into something.

Indun watched her friend turning on the tap on the sink and silently chuckled when she saw Siti vehemently shaking and squeezing the cleaning liquid.

"We ran out of cleaning liquid this morning," Indun pointed out.

Siti just looked at the empty bottle listlessly while holding a watery sponge, "Oh…"

"It's late now and the store is closed. But we can buy a new one tomorrow," Indun assured her friend, but then added humorously, "but this could have been easily solved if you worked at the convenient store next door, you know."

Siti's mind snapped back to where she was, standing in the living room of a big, old house, holding a phone to her ear. The memory of it all strengthened Siti's determination. Siti knew that she would receive an extra fee as compensation for her being willing to look after Mr. Jamuri's wife for the night. Siti thought that the money that she would get when Mr. Jamuri returned from his trip would be enough to cover her travel cost to Jakarta and to secure a cheap boarding house there. While still holding the receiver, Siti's eyes moved to read the dates on the wall calendar in front of her. She would only have to stay in this house until tomorrow. She asked Indun to buy two train tickets to Jakarta for that date. Siti figured that Indun had to come to Jakarta with her. Not only because Indun had practically become her surrogate family by this point, but also because Siti wanted to make sure that her best friend was safe, should Padil also decided to pay Indun a visit.

Indun agreed to buy the tickets this morning, "Hopefully there are still tickets left, 'Ti. It's near *Eid* day already and you know that by this time, most, if not all, train tickets must have been sold out." Siti took a deep breath. Her friend was right. It was already the third week of *Ramadan*, and usually, people would have already bought tickets for their trip to their family's hometown since the start of the holy month. She knew it was unlikely she would still be able to get tickets.

Indun, who seemed to sense Siti's concerns, said, "But don't worry. We only need two tickets, right? I think there is a good chance that they might still have them. I'll let you know how it goes. You don't have to worry about it." Then in an attempt to change the subject of their conversation, Indun asked, "How's Mrs. Surani doing?"

Siti sighed, "Her headache comes and goes, 'Ndun," Siti then proceeded by telling Indun that she had searched throughout all of the house and couldn't find any medicine left for the poor woman. Mr. Jamuri's place was quite big. Siti had heard that Mr. Jamuri was one of the richest people in the village and upon arriving there for the first time three weeks ago, she could attest to that rumour. While the house looked like it was stuck in the bygone era, it was filled with things that Siti could only dream of: furniture made out of solid wood, stone carvings on the walls, and vivid oil paintings that would make anyone stop and take notice.

"This is why I don't like big houses, 'Ti. If only he had kept his wife's medicine in our twenty-one-square-meter house, you would have found it right away," Indun joked.

Indun continued, being her usual chatty self, "Seriously, Ti, if someone asks me to live in a remote village, even if I am being gifted with a big house like that, I would still choose to live somewhere else. There are a lot of big cottonwood trees there, right?"

Siti remembered the large cottonwood tree that stood just across Mrs. Surani's window. "Yeah, there's a pretty big one by the main bedroom window."

She heard Indun laugh, "Well, just be careful, okay? I heard that the *Kuntilanak* likes to live in a large old cottonwood tree."

"It's not funny, Ndun," Siti said. In her head she pictured a female ghost in white clothes with long black hair flowing down to her ankles, sitting on an old tree branch, hunting for children who roam outside their house at night, to take as her own. The ghost stories told by her late mother when Siti was little to make her return home after sunset still managed to make her shudder.

She heard Indun laugh again. "Maybe Mr. Jamuri owns a *Kuntilanak* in that cottonwood tree, 'Ti. Legend says owning a *Kuntilanak* would make you rich."

""Ndun, if you keep carry on like this, I'll hang up, okay?" Siti grumbled, even though she knew she would never do such a thing.

Indun's laughter slowly faded, but she didn't change the subject immediately. In fact, her tone sounded serious now. She asked if the curtains on the window of Mrs. Surani's room were open. Siti remembered the dark red curtains on Mrs. Surani's window were drawn back, displaying the front yard, "Yes. She likes to sleep with the window curtains open so some light can come in."

A couple of seconds passed as if Indun was deliberating whether to say what was on her mind, before finally advising Siti to close the curtains on Mrs. Surani's bedroom window.

"I'm just saying, 'Ti. It is possible that someone, or *something*, that she sees outside made her ill."

"You mean because of the *Kuntilanak* in the cottonwood tree?" Siti couldn't hold back the annoyance in her voice.

"*Kuntilanak* is often possessive over her master and could make the master's wife ill or die if she wants to," Indun replied matter-of-factly. If she was still joking, Siti didn't sense any trace of it.

Suddenly Siti heard Mrs. Surani moaning again from her room, giving her an excuse to end the conversation. Again she reminded Indun not to forget to buy the train tickets this afternoon before replacing the receiver and walking towards Mrs. Surani's room.

Siti saw that Mrs. Surani was still sitting with her back against the headboard. The woman's gaze was directed at the window which revealed a large cottonwood tree in the yard against the dark sky. There was a dirt path in front of the house which was lit up by the pale yellowish light from the lamp on the side of the road. Siti could see the silhouettes of several people walking past Mr. Jamuri 's house towards the mosque near the village square. It was quarter past four, and Siti knew that some villagers went to the mosque to intensify their night prayers during the month of *Ramadan*. However, Siti realized that Mrs. Surani's gaze was locked on the old cottonwood tree which was right in front of her window.

"Mrs. Surani?" Siti called out.

The woman did not respond. Her eyes were fixed on that tree—or whatever resided in it. This made Siti remember what Indun had said on the phone a few minutes ago.

She likes to live in a large, old cottonwood tree. And she is often jealous of her master's wife.

Siti felt the hair on the back of her neck stand up. Almost unconsciously she moved towards the window and said, "I'll close the curtains, if that's okay, Ma'am, so you can rest… "

Suddenly, Mrs. Surani's voice was heard. "Leave it alone, my dear…," she sounded dispirited, not at all like how she was minutes ago, "I like to see people on the streets… "

"I have never been allowed to go outside by my husband," the woman lamented, "even though I really wanted to pray in the mosque like everyone else during *Ramadan*."

Siti's heart ached for the woman, "When you get better, I'm sure Mr. Jamuri will allow it, Ma'am. That's why you must take a lot of rest. Does your head still hurt?"

Mrs. Surani nodded as she touched the top of her head. Moaning in pain, she asked Siti to massage her head. Siti agreed and then climbed onto the bed, kneeling near Mrs. Surani. She gently helped the old woman reposition herself so that Mrs. Surani's back was facing her. Siti's fingers began to massage the woman's scalp with gentle pressure, as her late mother had taught her.

"Could you do it a little stronger, my dear?" Mrs. Surani asked, "I'm sorry, my hair is quite thick… I can't feel your hands if you don't apply more pressure."

Siti smiled as she massaged a little harder.

Mrs. Surani reminisced, “My friends used to make fun of me. They said ‘*Your hair is like a ghost’s hair*!”

The woman’s words reminded Siti of her conversation with Indun. Again her eyes were glued to the large tree in the yard as if something out there was forcing her to look.

“Ma’am …,” Siti heard herself speak in a hushed tone as if she was afraid that somebody else would hear, “I’ll just close the curtains, okay?”

Instead of responding to Siti, Mrs. Surani asked, “You’ve heard the stories often, haven’t you, child?”

Siti wasn’t sure about where the question was going, but then Mrs. Surani reminisced, “They say *she* likes to sit on a cottonwood tree every night. Often seduces every man who passes by and kidnaps children who are still roaming outside after dark.”

Siti tried to get rid of the image of the forsaken tree by the window from her view, but she couldn’t. She could see that Mrs. Surani’s eyes were also chained by the old tree. It was as if the thing that dwelled there wanted its presence to be known.

“Don’t look at the tree, Ma’am,” Siti whispered.

But it seems that Mrs. Surani did not listen because she just rambled on, as if under the influence of some malevolent force. But now there was contempt in her voice, “You’ve heard the story too, right, child? They say *Kuntilanak* can be *owned*.”

“Ma’am, *please* don’t look at that tree…,” Siti begged and finally acknowledged what she had feared to be true, “Don’t give her what she wants, Ma’am… She *wants* to be seen.” Fear overtook Siti and she began to cry.

“They say there is one way one can domesticate a *Kuntilanak*. Can you tell me how, child?”

Siti knew she didn't need to respond. Instead, she lowered her head, trying to avoid the ghastly image that was plastered outside the window, turning her gaze to her fingers that still rested on Mrs. Surani's head. But suddenly her tongue curled up by itself and replied, in between her sobs, "*By driving... by driving a nail into her head, Ma'am...*"

As the answer flew from her lips, Siti saw something that made her cry out.

A black steel nail head protruded from Mrs. Surani's crown.

Siti's body went limp. She fell backward on the bed, eyes locked at the back of the woman in front of her who sat there, as still as a rock. In an unnaturally ethereal voice, Mrs. Surani whispered, "*Could you please remove the nail from my head, child?*"

Siti could not answer. She could only stare at the long-haired woman who was sitting with her back to her, causing her to cry uncontrollably like that of a child.

"I can't take this off by myself," Mrs. Surani wailed again.

Siti screamed when she saw the woman—*the creature*—turned to her. Shades of blinding whites covered the entire surface of her eyes, making them look like a pair of twin moons floating in the dim light.

Mrs. Surani's whole body was now facing Siti. Like a reptile, she crawled on the bed, closer and closer. With her limestone-cold hand, she reached out and grabbed Siti's arm, scanning the bruises on the young woman's skin.

"He did this to me too... " she croaked, rubbing her cold fingers gently against the blue marks, *"I know exactly how you feel, child... "*

Her sorrowful lament quickly turned into rage as she hissed, "Those bastards. They think of us as their servants. Our tears, our blood, our lives mean nothing to them."

Finally, Mrs. Surani's withered face arrived right next to Siti's ear. "When he killed me and buried me under that cottonwood tree, I thought that I would be free from him. Turns out he still wants to keep me in chains, even after I die."

Siti felt a quiver in Mrs. Surani's voice, "Release me from him, child... Take this god-forsaken thing off of me then leave this cursed place."

Something odd rose in Siti's mind. She felt that she could understand Mrs. Surani's request. More than that, she thought that her yearning for freedom was reasonable. Even though Siti's heart was pounding in her ears, there was a glimmer of calm that enveloped her mind. Siti felt that if she could release the dead woman from the shackles that kept her earthbound, then Siti—a living, breathing woman—might have a chance of saving herself from Padil.

As if she could read Siti's thoughts, Mrs. Surani stuck her head out in a snake-like movement, revealing the crown where the rusty nail had lodged. Siti's hands reached for the nail-head—how she did it she will never know. Then she gripped the nail head firmly with her sweat-drenched fingers and began to move it left and right.

The spike gave in more easily than she thought. A bubbling torrent of black blood gushed out of the hole in Mrs. Surani's head. Siti screamed but did not release her grip. She twisted and pulled to pry the nail out. The sooty black liquid gave off a foul stench engulfing everything in its path. Siti could feel those fluids entering her eyelids, staining her teeth, lodging themselves under the pores of her tongue. Siti vomited a hoarse scream as she pulled the black spike out, freed from its tomb. Siti's back crashed onto the mattress which was soaked with blood. Along with Siti's roar, Mrs. Surani emitted a guttural laugh. Every cackle in her voice was so piercingly sharp that it felt like it could slash Siti's eardrums.

Siti was too drained to make sense of everything that was happening. But she remembered Mrs. Surani's glowing white eyes staring at her intently for the last time, as if engraving Siti in her eternal memory, before finally floating swiftly away through the window. The *Kuntilanak* soared in the night sky, squealing her laughter as a free woman, just as the sound of the call to dawn prayer rose up from the nearby mosque.

Siti's ears caught the frightened screams of the villagers, all of whom were in disarray, witnessing a woman who finally tasted the joy of disobedience only after she was dead. However, Siti knew that it was not the villagers who were going to suffer the brunt of the siren's wrath.

In her exhaustion, Siti could imagine the creature returning to its nesting place in the cottonwood tree by the window, waiting for the return of the man who had taken her life.

Siti closed her eyes for a moment, letting the symphony of screams throughout the village echo in her ears, possessing her every being. She knew she was destined to be free, just like the lady up the cottonwood tree.

AFTERWORD

First of all, thank you for purchasing *Who's There? (A Collection of Stories)*. I know you could have picked any number of books to read, but you picked this one, and for that I am extremely grateful.

I want you, the reader, to know that I value your opinion greatly. If you enjoyed this book, I'd like to hear from you, and hope that you could take some time to post a review on Goodreads or Amazon, so that others can enjoy the same experience you have. Your review will also help me to see what is and isn't working, so I can better serve you and all my other readers in the future. If you would like to leave a review, all you have to do is visit Amazon or Goodreads and away you go.

Again, thank you, and I wish you all the best in your future success!

ABOUT THE AUTHOR

Dimas Rio is an Indonesian-born legal counsel and fiction writer who has been treading between two worlds since his college days. He published his first novel, *Dinner with Saucer* in 2007 during his last year at law school, which went on to be shortlisted in Indonesia's *Khatulistiwa Literary Award* of 2007 in the Talented Young Writer category.

He first self-published *Who's There? (A Collection of Stories)* in 2019 which received recognition from notable publications, namely *Kirkus Reviews* which described it as "entrancing and unnerving". The book was subsequently re-published by Velox Books, a US based publisher focusing on creepy and intriguing short stories.

Aside from writing, his hobbies include cooking and baking, singing when nobody's watching, reading, and making book review videos on YouTube under the name of Kelinting Reads.

Dimas can be contacted on his Instagram account @dimas_riyo

Printed in Great Britain
by Amazon